GIRL ON A PLANE

GIRL ON A PLANE

MIRIAM MOSS

ANDERSEN PRESS

This book is a work of fiction based on the author's own experiences.
The names and identifying characteristics of individuals are entirely fictional.
Though based on a real-life hijacking, dialogue, characters and incidents have been
fictionalised, and some time frames have been compressed to convey the story.
Please read the postscript on pages 262–263 for further information.

First published in 2015 by
Andersen Press Limited
20 Vauxhall Bridge Road
London SW1V 2SA
www.andersenpress.co.uk

2 4 6 8 10 9 7 5 3 1

'The vastest things are those we may not learn' from *Peake's Progress* by Mervyn
Peake reprinted by permission of Peters Fraser & Dunlop on behalf of the Estate of
Mervyn Peake

British Library Cataloguing in Publication Data available.

ISBN 978 1 78344 331 4

Printed and bound by
CPI Group (UK) Ltd, Croydon, CR0 4YY

For my family and in memory of my father and mother

The vastest things are those we may not learn.
We are not taught to die or to be born
Nor how to burn
With love.
How pitiful is our enforced return
To those small things we are the masters of.

Mervyn Peake

1

Tuesday 8th September 1970

Bahrain - 14.00 hrs

A Forces child, that's what they call me.

It's all I've ever known: living in rented houses and moving every few years to a different country. So being here in Bahrain, on this small teardrop of an island in the Persian Gulf, feels normal.

Moving so often means leaving friends, starting new schools halfway through term and being the new girl over and over again. Catching up with schoolwork can be a struggle too, so when I was eleven my parents decided to send me to boarding school back in England. Now I travel out to see them in the holidays, when they can afford it.

My dad's in the army. And my mother, who I've always called Marni, is a primary school teacher.

It's the last day of the summer holidays, and tomorrow I'm leaving Bahrain for ever because we're moving again. My two younger brothers are travelling back to school a couple of days after me, and my parents will go at the end of the week.

Dad's been stationed back in England for a while. We won't be coming out to Bahrain again.

I'm meant to be packing, but I refuse to engage. I'm staying put, right here on the roof, lying in the shade next to Woofa, our dog, and stroking his golden ears. He is looking at me with puzzled, toffee-coloured eyes that say, *So how come* I'm *suddenly allowed up here?*

The house roof is flat with a chest-high wall round it. It's where we all come to catch the breeze. And on unbearably hot nights we're even allowed to sleep up here. Then the light in the pink sky, and the doves cooing in the date palms and the muezzin calling everyone to prayer wake us early. By seven the sun's so hot you have to go back inside anyway.

The walls were once painted a blinding white. Now they're smudged and pockmarked from the blows of endless cricket balls and footballs, especially around the goalmouth and the stumps my father painted on for the boys. The only things left up here now, stacked against the wall, are two green sunloungers. When you open them up, the sharp cogs pinch your fingers and the metal frame burns your bare skin.

Woofa is sending me waves of sympathy, like only dogs can. He knows that all I have to look forward to now are school and exams. He knows we're leaving. He's known for a while. He attached himself to our family after being abandoned by his previous one, so he's seen it all before.

I lift one of his ears. The inside looks like curled pasta. 'You'll be all right, Woofa,' I say. 'You only have to move next door this time, to live with the Adelmans. They're really nice.' Mrs Adelman is American and once taught me how to make cookies, half plain, half chocolate, in a roll that you cut slices off and then bake.

'Anna!'

Oh dear. Marni. I put my arms round Woofa's neck and bury my face in the thick fur of his ruff, but then, hearing my mother's footsteps on the stairs, I get up quickly.

'There you are!' Her eyes slide down to rest on Woofa. 'Oh, Anna,' she says. Woofa sidles guiltily past her and down the stairs. '*You*,' she says to me, 'are very naughty.' Her frown is disapproving, but her dark eyes don't mean it.

'I know.' I smile at her. 'I am.' She puts a firm arm round my shoulders, turns me and gently guides me down the stairs in front of her.

But I still don't go to pack. I sit down at the dining-room table beside Sam, my nine-year-old brother. He's drawn what I think is a hippo and is colouring it in purple.

'Anna?' Marni says, as I settle down next to him.

'I'll go in a minute. I promise,' I say. 'That's really good, Sam.' He carries on, concentrating, the tip of his tongue between his lips. The overhead fan whooshes the smells of woodchip and furniture polish around the room and flutters the pile of newspapers that Marni's using to wrap up the glasses. She picks up a water jug, rolls it in Arabic newsprint and packs it carefully into the silver foil-lined crate. She's done this so many times before. Her brown hands move quickly, her engagement ring catching the light.

'At the party last night,' I say, 'they said loads of planes have been hijacked.' My words hang in the air. The date-palm fronds finger the windowpane, like they're trying to get in.

Marni rips a sheet of newspaper in half. 'Ignore them,' she says. 'They're just trying to unsettle you before you fly.'

'No, Marni, they really have,' I insist. 'Everyone was talking about it. They were all teasing me, saying it'd be my turn

3

tomorrow. It was quite funny really...'

Marni looks straight at me, her eyes intense. What Dad calls her *still waters run deep* eyes. 'Well, *you* aren't going to be hijacked.'

She reaches for the yellow-and-terracotta vase they bought in Venice on their honeymoon and starts wrapping it.

'No, you're right, I probably won't be.' I turn to Sam. 'Maybe you will instead.'

'Anna!' Marni shoots me a look.

'What does hijacked mean?' Sam pipes up, pulling a black crayon from the box and scribbling on a whiskery tail.

'Anna's being silly, darling. It hardly ever happens, and usually no one gets hurt.'

'But what *is* it?' he insists.

'It's when people hold up a plane to make it go somewhere else,' she says. Then she turns to me. 'Now, have you got enough envelopes to write home with?' I don't respond to this unsubtle attempt to get me to pack. I want to see if she'll say, *Anna, it's time to gird up your loins.* Or her favourite: *Anna, I'm going to have to put a bomb under you.* But it's neither. She just says, 'How much pocket money do you think you'll need this term?' And that's when I know she's heard about the hijackings too. She's thinking that we all have to fly this week, and doesn't want us to be worried about it, especially me, as I'll be travelling alone. Anyway, she said it hardly ever happens, so I suppose I'll probably be fine.

She tries another tack. 'You know Dad brought your school uniform back from the cleaners when he came home for lunch?' She pauses. 'It's on your bed, ready to pack.'

That's hard, really hard. Now *it's* here, I can't pretend any more, and she knows it. Now I have to face the facts.

I really am leaving tomorrow.

I wander into my room. And there it is, lying under transparent plastic: one brown tweed skirt – box pleats, regulation knee-length – matching brown regulation sack coat with horn buttons, fawn cardigan, itchy woollen games culottes, specially designed to give you nappy rash. I stuff it all out of sight, right down at the bottom of my case next to my granny-style school shoes. I'm not wearing *that* stuff on the plane. I'll change into it at the last possible moment, probably in the back of the taxi going to school from the station.

I put my travelling clothes out on my chair instead: a cream wrapover miniskirt, bronze T-shirt and the wide black silver-buckled belt I bought in Chelsea Girl last term. Then I slump down on the bed. I can't bear it. I won't see my family again until the end of term, fifteen whole weeks away, and that'll be in yet another new place where I won't know anyone at all. Again.

I roll over and curl up. A wave of homesickness washes through me, and just when I'm feeling *really* desperate I hear Woofa's tail wagging against the end of my bed. He comes alongside and leans his snout sympathetically on the edge of the sheet. 'Oh, Woofa,' I say. 'Please think of something that will stop me having to go back to school.'

He nuzzles my hand, but there's nothing he or anyone can do to stop the inevitable.

2

Wednesday 9th September 1970

09.00 hrs

They're loading my case into the car.

I dash up onto the roof to have one last look over the balustrade, across the wasteground stretching to the blue-domed mosque with its two white minarets. I will never ever live here again. I will never lie here with Marni, slightly tipsy after the Adelmans' Pimm's party, crying with laughter at something neither of us can remember the next day.

I clatter downstairs and out into the front garden to find Woofa. He's lying in the shade under the old palm tree, near where we found the abandoned litter of puppies. I hug him one last time, choking back my tears, seeing his sad eyes saying he knows it's the end. Then I run through the blurring house, past my parents' bedroom where once Dad flung out his arm and smashed the bedside lamp while having a nightmare. Into the hall, past the open airing cupboard where the fresh towels lie in rounded stacks, past the bathroom where the dodgy light with the loose connection electrocuted me. Past the cutlery drawer in the hall lined with baize and smelling of lacquer, under the arch into the sitting room, where Dad's new tape deck blasts out Harry Belafonte, and the chorister at Christmas always sings, 'Once in Royal David's City'. Past ghost marks on the wall where the pictures used to hang. Finally I say goodbye to the tall cream fridge that hums and wheezes all through the night.

I close the back door. The mosquito frame bangs shut behind me. Marni is standing by the Peugeot wearing her turquoise shirtdress and a matching silk scarf. She ties the scarf in a knot at the back, but it never manages to contain her coppery curls. The boys are already bouncing around in the back of the car. Dad pointedly revs the engine. Marni and I climb in.

She glances down at the man's watch she always wears halfway up her arm. 'You'll have to put your foot down,' she says, 'or we'll miss the flight.'

'*Anna's going to miss her flight!*' the boys chant over and over until Marni hushes them. We judder down the potholed dust track and out onto the tarmac road. And we're off under the blue Bahraini sky, tilting as we circle the roundabout to take the airport road to Muharraq.

The hot wind, smelling of goats, drains and exhaust fumes, buffets in through the open windows. Marni's scarf tails dance wildly, as if struggling to escape. The king palms lining the road shiver and toss their heads, trying to shake off the sea breeze. Suddenly there's a whiff of cardamom, reminding me of the glasses of tea the shopkeepers offer in the souk.

'Must be well over a hundred degrees out there already,' Dad shouts above the noise of the broken exhaust. And I feel beads of sweat gathering. They trickle down my spine and pool in the small of my back.

As we cross the causeway to the airport, everyone in the car goes quiet. I know this quiet. It's full of dread, the dread of us being separated. We're all thinking the same thing: it's all change again. None of us wants it, but what can we do? I feel a terrible heaviness, the sort you get just before tears come.

When we finally park, Dad grabs my case and we run in a straggle across tarmac softened by the intense heat. And I think how the impression of my footprints will be the only thing left of me in Bahrain.

Marni pulls open the swing doors to the departures hall, Dad heaves my case inside and I feel a cold blast of air conditioning. We slow to a walk, stop panting and start to fit in with the quieter throng milling about on the concourse.

'*Salaam alaikum.*' Dad greets the man wearing a turquoise BOAC uniform at the check-in desk. Marni passes over my ticket. The man tears out the duplicate flight page and gives it back. I watch my case being weighed. I'm here and not here, in a daze, feeling condemned.

'Now, don't you go losing that, will you?' Dad says, handing me the ticket. His teasing is meant to raise my spirits. When I don't answer, he looks down at me again, his grey eyes questioning.

'I'm fifteen, Dad. Done this loads of times,' I say flatly.

'I know.' He smiles and puts his arm around me. 'But you'll always be my little girl.' I can smell his Old Spice aftershave. I look for the patch under his bottom lip that he always misses when he shaves. There it is.

The boys stand on either side of Marni, solemn as statues.

'You're lucky, Anna,' Mark says. 'You don't have to wear a stupid *Unaccompanied Child* label any more, like we do.'

'No.' I ruffle his sun-streaked hair. 'I'm a big girl now.'

'*Unaccompanied Child.*' Sam says it slowly, looking up at Marni. 'Like we're *orphans*.'

She's stung. 'Well, you aren't, and you know you aren't. You all know exactly why this is necessary – and how horrible it is for all of us.' Her voice breaks slightly.

'Come on now, you boys.' Dad is all forced bonhomie. 'Let's wave Anna through the gate.'

A blonde girl in front of us, older than me, clings to her mother, weeping. Her mother pats her back once, very quickly, as if she mustn't, as if it's no longer allowed. They move, walking as if through deep sand, towards the gate where her sister stands palely by their father.

I hate this next bit more than anything. Marni says to do it very quickly. No point dragging it out. So I walk up to her. She puts her arms round me, and for a moment I'm in that soft, safe place where I can always be just me, with the smell of her, her lipstick, her Pond's cream and Je Reviens perfume.

'Stay safe, my most precious girl,' she says, stroking my head instinctively just above the ear, as she always does. Then she kisses me and pushes me gently away. I turn, tears streaming, to hug the boys. They come both together, their arms tight round my waist. Then I hug Dad quickly, and walk away.

I turn once; see the boys' tears, Dad's frown and Marni's terrible distorted smile. And for a moment I waver.

'Go!' she says. But I stay, trying to absorb them, burning them onto my mind's eye. Then I turn away and walk, holding up one hand, waving without looking.

The tall boy in front of me in the queue waiting to board looks constantly back over my head. He's ashen-faced with tension. I hand my ticket to the man at the gate, show my passport, heft my shoulder bag and walk past the neat, smiling air hostess.

My bag thumps against my thigh as I walk out across the tarmac to the waiting plane. It's a white VC10 with a high tail and 'BOAC' written in huge navy-blue letters down its body. I've never flown completely alone before, not without the boys, or a friend. Anxiously I recheck the ticket in my hand. 'BOAC', it says across the front. *All over the world, the British Overseas Aircraft Corporation takes good care of you.*

3

10.30 hrs

A camel just beyond the perimeter fence wobbles in the heat as the plane's engines rage briefly. There's a surge as we begin to move forward, then I'm thrust back in my seat as the tarmac races. I feel the slant and lift as the front wheel, then the back, leave the ground, and I imagine them spinning as the earth falls away.

The plane circles over the grey-gold desert spotted with date palms and climbs into the blue. When it drops in a pocket of thin air everyone gasps – then there's a ripple of nervous laughter.

I think of Marni standing below in her silk scarf and dark glasses. She'll wait till the plane is a tiny speck, then she'll take the boys' hands. They'll ask for a Pepsi on the way home, and she'll say yes because she'll be waving them off soon.

I sit back, resigned to being on my own for the next seven hours. It'll be early afternoon when we land. London's two hours behind Bahrain. The pretty air hostess who greeted us as we boarded comes to offer the little boy on my right a child's pack of crayons and a colouring book. Her badge says *Rosemary.*

They've obviously put the kids travelling alone all together. I'm about four rows back from the curtain into first class, between two boys. On my other side is the one who was in front of me in the queue. It's not ideal, but better than on the way out, when I was squeezed next to a massively overweight man with bad breath.

I pull the safety card from the seat pocket in front and look at the diagrams: the emergency position, how to break open the windows, how to slide down the chutes into the ocean, only, obviously, after removing your high heels. I shove it back in my seat pocket and stare out of the little round porthole at the empty sky. God, I really am on my way. No going back now. No more bikinis and flip-flops. No more water-skiing or skinny-dipping off dhows, or barbeques on sandbanks in the middle of the sea.

But this is grim. I need to think about something uplifting. Marni has a habit of throwing negative thoughts away. Literally. She did a classic yesterday after I'd packed. She came into my room jangling the car keys and said it was time to go shoe shopping, compensation for going back to school. I jumped up and followed her to the car. 'Imagine just having to wear my hideous school lace-ups for the next three years,' I said as we drove.

'Awful,' she agreed. 'They really wouldn't look out of place on a parade ground. But, come on, let's not think about school lace-ups, let's throw the thought of *them* away.' So we both wound down our windows, and threw the imaginary shoes out. It's what Marni always does to get rid of troublesome things:

like coughs, annoying thoughts, bad-tempered people.

Not easy in here though . . .

I pull the flight magazine out of the seat pocket and start flicking through it.

'It's full of crap,' the boy on my left says suddenly. 'I just looked.'

I smile quickly at him. *Glossy brown hair, sporty, seventeen?*

'Going back to school?' His voice is almost a drawl.

'Yes. Just to catch up on some sleep.'

He laughs. *Strong white teeth.* Not sure I want this right now.

'Which school?' he says, pushing his fringe out of his eyes.

I grimace. 'St Saviour's, Barchester. All *gels*.'

'Sounds great.' His hands lie relaxed on his thighs.

'For you, maybe,' I say. *I've met ones like this before. A charmer.*

'Mine's all boys, in Bristol.' He brushes the end of his nose with his fingers, as if a fly just landed there.

'Nice.'

I look over at the small boy on my other side. He's about nine, the same age as Sam, wearing an *Unaccompanied* badge and staring out of the window, a big square cake tin cradled on his lap. I nod at the tin. 'That your tuckbox?' It has holly and a snow scene on it.

He looks up at me with solemn brown eyes. 'No. It's my terrapin.'

'Really?'

'Yes.' His nose is sprinkled with freckles and he has short ginger hair with an off-centre cowlick.

'You taking it back to school?'

'Yes.' He says it quickly before looking back out of the window.

13

'Can I see it?' I ask gently.

He hesitates, then prises off the lid. Inside, in a slop of water filled with pondweed, is a little striped green-and-yellow terrapin about the size of his hand. It tilts its pointed snout and stares crossly at me.

'Oh,' I say. 'Nice markings.' The boy looks up at me gratefully. There's something fragile about his heart-shaped face.

'Will it be OK in there?'

'There are holes in the top,' he points to them, 'so he can breathe. Dad made them.'

I smile. 'What's his name? I mean the terrapin, not your dad.'

'Fred.'

I lean down. 'Hello, Fred,' I whisper at the fierce little snout. Fred slowly lifts one striped leg free of weed, his slit eyes brimming with disdain.

'You're so lucky,' I say. 'I wish I could have my dog here on board. I had to leave him . . .' I trail off, overwhelmed.

But then, not wanting to upset the little boy, I pull myself together. 'Did anyone say anything when you checked in?'

'Dad asked them. They said it was all right.'

'That's good. I saw an Arab at the airport once with a bird of prey on his arm, you know, with a hood on, and a bell . . .'

'Christ!' The older boy next to me is staring rigidly ahead. The curtain between first class and the main cabin has been thrust aside by a young Arab.

He's holding a gun.

4

11.30 hrs

The plane's roar fills my head.

The man's eyes are wild. The gun in his hand shakes. 'Sit in your seats!' he screams. We sit, still as stone.

I'm in a film, on a movie set. I must be. It can't be real...I...

The man is sweating. He twists his mouth to wipe it with the back of his free hand.

But the gun, the gun...

Someone behind me cries out. The man waves his gun wildly in their direction.

I shrink down in my seat, stare at the hands in my lap. They're my hands, my real hands. There's the freckle on my finger. If the gun goes off, we'll all be sucked out. Oh my God! Oh my God!

My heart thunders. I close my eyes, hear shallow breathing.

Suddenly the intercom crackles overhead: '*Ladies and gentlemen, this is Captain Gregory speaking. I'm sorry to have to inform you that we've been hijacked by the Popular Front for the Liberation of Palestine.'* There's murmuring, then silence.

Hijacked? Like those other planes. But one of them blew up. Tom said so at the party on Monday night. Fear rages in my gut. We're all going to die.

A deep Arab voice takes over. *'Your captain says he is sorry! But we are not sorry! We are the PFLP. We are trying to free Palestine!'* There's a pause.

The captain returns, talking slowly, as if speaking to foreigners. *'Ladies and gentlemen, I hope you're all all right. I have been asked to tell you that we have a hijacker in the cockpit, as well as the one in the cabin. They're insisting we fly to Beirut to refuel, then to their Revolutionary Airstrip in the Jordanian desert.'* He pauses. *'It's very important that we all stay calm and obey these people. So please stay in your seats. It'll take about an hour to get to Beirut. I'll keep you informed of developments, I promise, as soon as I know more. Ladies and gentlemen, boys and girls, I repeat, please stay calm. I'll speak to you again shortly.'*

Sweat trickles from the gunman's temple. His hand still shakes as he waves the gun over and back.

I mustn't move. No one must move.

The boys on either side are dead still, the little one curled up against the window. The silence in the cabin is all wrong. The colour of bile. He's going to kill someone. I close my eyes. Try not to panic. My mind flits and darts – and then begins to drift...

This has nothing to do with me...I'm in a dream...I know it's a dream...I don't know how I know...I don't care, somewhere inside...a tidal wave of fear...it hasn't hit yet...but it's coming.

And in the stillness, in the yawning, white silence, I feel a terrible calm.

So this is what happens when you're going to die...

Die?

I snap back.

He's still there, turning his head tortoise-like, this way and that, his close-set eyes flicking round the cabin. The gun swings and points. Fear fills my throat. Tears rise. The boys on either side are hardly breathing. I don't move my head. I just see their hands in their laps, the edge of my maroon shoes. The ones Marni bought yesterday. *I'm going to die in them.*

Oh God. Marni.

A woman behind me starts to sob.

The little boy leans very slowly towards me and says quietly, 'Where did the captain say we're going?'

I keep my eyes on the gun. 'Jordan,' I whisper. 'He said Jordan. You all right?'

He nods, but moves his arm close to mine. It's trembling.

'What's your name?' I say, staring ahead.

'Tim.'

'I'm Anna. Don't worry. I'm sure this will all be over soon.' I feel the boy on the other side tense.

Huge sweat rings bloom under the hijacker's arms. His black hair lies slicked down over his forehead.

Suddenly his bulging eyes stare directly at me. I go hot, cold, concentrate on the cream chairback in front. There's a stain there shaped like a boot.

'Who *is* that man?' Tim asks. 'What does he want?'

I wait till the hijacker looks the other way, then lean forward and duck below the seat, so that he can't see my head. 'He's a Palestinian, Tim,' I whisper. 'They were chucked off their land in a war, and I think they're trying to get it back. They're taking us to an airstrip in the desert.' And I remember my friend Samir taking me into his dad's study a few days ago, to show me pictures of where he used to live in Palestine, in a white house surrounded by olive groves.

'I have a friend,' I whisper, 'who used to live in Palestine.'

The little boy looks at me. 'Is your friend a hijacker too?'

'No,' I say. 'Not all Palestinians are hijackers. His family fled during the war with Israel when he was younger. Luckily his dad got a job in Bahrain.'

'Ladies and gentlemen, boys and girls. This is Captain Gregory again. Thank you for remaining calm. I've been asked by the two hijackers to tell you that there's another member of the PFLP, sitting in the aisle seat in Row 20 holding a black briefcase full of explosives.'

I hear gasps. People look round, trying to spot the hijacker. A bolt of panic shoots through me. I feel cold, sick.

Tim touches my arm. 'Why has he got explosives? Is he going to blow us up?'

Coils of fear squirm in my gut. I try to keep my voice steady. 'He'd be blowing himself up too then. So I expect it's just a threat to make us do as they say.'

I can't do this. I can't. Please, let me put my head down on my table. Let me close my eyes. Let me go to sleep.

'Are you scared?' Tim asks, with the ghost of a breath.

'Yes,' I say. 'I am a bit.'

'Me too.' He stares ahead. He's very good at being quiet. Must be practice. Boarding school after lights out.

'We'll be all right,' I say. I turn a little and look at him, attempt a smile.

I try not to look at the jittery hijacker again. Instead I stare through the gap in the seats in front. It's only a few inches wide, but I can see the armrests, each with a metal fliptop ashtray cut into it, all the way to the bulkhead at the front. The arms resting on them are all still.

I glance quickly at the boy on my other side. He's sitting stiffly with his head back, his eyes closed. An Arab man sitting across the aisle, with his wife and child, twists round a little in his seat, looking down the aisle for the man with the explosives, I suspect. But then he glances up at Sweaty and thinks better of it.

'*Ladies and gentlemen.*' It's the captain again. '*If we are to stay safe, we must remain calm, keep quiet and do exactly what the hijackers say – or, they say, they will detonate the bomb. Now, in a minute the hijackers will come through the cabin. They want you to hand in your passports, open at your picture for them to check. After they've been stamped with the Revolutionary Airport stamp, they say they will be returned to you. Please co-operate with them, and please remain quiet and calm. I'll speak to you all again soon.*'

A giant of a man suddenly pushes through the curtain with a machine gun slung over one shoulder. His broad face, framed with thick curly hair and a dark beard, is tense. Businesslike, he begins collecting passports from the passengers at the front, piling them up in his huge hands. He looks strangely detached, as if he's just going through the motions.

As he begins to make his way down the cabin, we all scrabble around looking for our passports, and it feels good to be doing something. I drag my shoulder bag from where it lies slumped at my feet. The older boy is already turning his passport over and over in his hands. He puts it down on his lap, picks it up again, opens it at the photo. I read his name.

'David,' I say.

'Yes.' He turns and looks through me, his voice miles away.

'I'm Anna,' I say quietly. 'He's Tim.' Tim raises his hand in a half-wave.

David looks at us, as if perplexed, then back down at his passport.

'Have you found yours?' I ask Tim. He nods. 'And Fred's?'

He looks up at me, his eyes bright. '*He* hasn't got one, silly!'

Suddenly the hijacker's machine gun clunks against David's seat. He's wearing a bullet belt. I've never seen one so close up. The bullets look polished, *contained*. And sharp, and puncturing. I see shards of twisted metal in bloody flesh, in shattered bones.

The giant hijacker stops to tidy his pile of passports. I'm shocked by his immaculately clean hands, his square fingernails, the dark wrist hair curling around his metal watchstrap. His jeans and white T-shirt look so ordinary. Washed and ironed. He's made of flesh and blood. And yet he might kill us.

He takes David's passport, looks straight at me, smiles grimly and holds out a huge hand. As I give him my passport, my fingers brush his and I pull back, electrified.

He takes Tim's and moves on down through the cabin.

'Did you see?' Tim whispers. 'His head nearly touched the ceiling.'

'Yes,' I say. 'One's a giant, and the other one is seriously sweaty.'

'Charming pair,' David mutters.

We fall silent as the sweaty one brushes past to go to the back of the plane. When it's clear again, I ask David if he can see the man with the bomb.

'It's Row 20,' I say. 'About ten back.'

David twists round and looks down the aisle. 'There's just a foot sticking out. A black lace-up.' He turns to me.

'He's probably wearing a suit.'

'The boss, you think?'

He shrugs. The Giant and Sweaty walk back up into first class, loaded with passports.

'Weird,' David says. 'Everyone was talking about hijackings, but I never thought it would happen to me. Stupid, really.'

'I know,' I say. 'People were teasing me about it too, but I didn't think it could actually happen. Why d'you think they want our passports?

'To find out who we all are, where we come from, I suppose. They're probably looking for Israelis.'

'Why?' Tim asks.

David leans forward. 'The PFLP hijacked four planes on Sunday, all heading for America. Two of them have been taken to a place in the Jordanian desert. Another one, a Pan Am flight, got blown up in Cairo after everyone had got off.'

'And the fourth?' I ask.

'That was an Israeli plane, El Al. The two hijackers on that one were overcome by the crew. The plane made an emergency landing at Heathrow. One hijacker was killed, the other's in prison in London. But that's the plane the PFLP really wanted, the one from Israel.'

'Why?' Tim asks again.

'It was the Israelis, they say, who drove them off their land.'

5

12.30 hrs

As our plane hums on and on towards Beirut, David takes a battered James Bond paperback from the webbed seat pocket in front of him. Tim follows suit, pulling a Paddington Bear story from his satchel. I look at them in disbelief. How can they think of reading with all this going on? But they do.

In the end, and reluctantly, I take *Wuthering Heights* from my bag. It's a set text and I should have read it and made notes over the holidays. But of course I was too busy having a good time. That was then.

I try hard to concentrate but my eyes keep glazing over. I'm reading the same line again and again. So instead I listen to the throb of the plane, to David turning a page, to the man talking quietly to the woman behind. She's stopped sobbing now and only occasionally gives a great juddering sigh.

The hijackers have allowed the crew to get up. They've tied back the blue curtain between us and first class, so now I can see a few of the passengers in the left aisle seats there. They're being tended to by the chief steward. He's handing a whisky to a large bald man smoking a cigar. The girl behind with red-blonde hair and a short cropped top is frantically filing her nails with an emery board. I stare at the two red-and-white Exit signs on either side of the curtains. Exit. What a strange word. And where precisely can we exit *to*? There *is* no exit now. Not *that* kind.

I might die up here, walled in between rows and rows of seats.

The thought makes me feel sick and panicky again, so I push it away and watch the man and woman directly in front turning to whisper to each other. I can see the colour of her eyes (blue) and the black hairs in his nostrils. If I put out my hand, I could touch her cheekbone.

I'm feeling restless and claustrophobic. The chair fabric is hot and prickly under my bare legs, and my arms are cramped in to my body. David's taking up most of the space on our armrest and Tim's resting Fred's tin on the other one. I long to stretch out. If I did, one arm would touch the window and the other the far edge of David's seat. Instead I reach up towards the low ceiling as if to change the nozzle on the air-conditioner cone. My fingertips only just graze the light button. Next I push my legs out and swing them up under the seat in front. I can feel the soft life jacket. It's crazy, but knowing it's there makes me feel a little better.

Tim shifts the tin onto his lap, so I rest my arm on the armrest and fiddle with the built-in ashtray, opening and shutting the lid. There's a pile of old grey ash in there. The smell of it wafts up. David stops reading, holds his book between his knees, marking his place with a finger, and frowns at me. I stop playing with the ashtray. He goes back to his book. I notice that the woman in front has her hair fixed back with brown kirby grips; they remind me of Marni.

Does Marni know? What will she say when she does?

Marni, I'm being hijacked. The words rush round my head. Unleashed. Impossible to absorb. *You said it hardly ever happened. But it has. Don't let the boys fly tomorrow, Marni. Stay there. All of you. Don't fly.* The woman behind lets out one of her juddering sighs. *Will I ever see you again, Marni? If I die, will it hurt?*

Fear prickles my skin. Tears rise. A sob grips me.

'I HAVE TO GO!' a man shouts from behind. 'I MUST GO!' he bellows. 'I HAVE TO USE THE TOILET! I MUST BE ALLOWED TO USE...'

'SIT IN YOUR SEAT!' Sweaty's voice, high and shrill, rises over his. The three of us turn round to watch, half kneeling on our seats. Sweaty charges towards the middle-aged man standing in the aisle and pushes him roughly down in his seat. The man stands back up, his face red and flustered, his grey hair tousled. There's a scuffle. The woman behind me covers her face. The man with the bomb briefcase lifts it to his chest, hugs it like it's precious. The Giant strides down the aisle towards Sweaty. Both hijackers train their guns on the standing man.

I turn away, can't watch, shut my eyes, wait for the shots.

The cabin will de-pressurise. We'll all be sucked out.

My hands clutch the seat. *FOR GOD'S SAKE, SIT DOWN*, I scream inside. The fear in my chest, tightening like a vice, takes my breath away.

The plane hangs in space.

There's a flurry of air as Rosemary the air hostess walks down the aisle with her hands up. 'Let me help,' she says. 'Please, let me help.' Her voice is clear and reasonable and calm. 'The passengers will need to go to the toilets.' She keeps talking. 'What about letting them go one by one? I'll go with them. It's not a trick, I promise. I'll make sure nothing happens.'

I climb back up again to peer over the back of my seat. Tim and David are half standing. The hijackers' guns point at Rosemary now.

'Wait here!' the Giant says, squeezing past her. He strides back to the man with the bomb briefcase and talks quietly in Arabic to him. Rosemary persuades the passenger to sit down.

The Giant marches back down the aisle. 'One only,' he says to Rosemary, holding up a finger. 'With you. Only one at a time.'

'Thank you.' She reaches out to the seated man. 'Come this way.' He stands and she follows him down the aisle to the toilets at the back.

The man with the briefcase places it down by his feet.

I sit back down.

David looks at me, his face ashen. 'We're trapped inside a huge metal bomb.'

'What if someone else does something really stupid?' I say.

'Well, that'll be it,' David says. 'He'll blow us up. Christ.' He looks away. 'This is shit.'

I can't speak. My tray clatters down. I put my elbows on it and rest my head in my hands. *Any minute. Die here surrounded by strangers. Disappear. Become nothing.*

The hard lump of fear in my chest flickers and glows... blazes. Tears sting my eyes. *Endless nothing...*

Stop. STOP IT. Breathe. Just breathe. Say something calm. Calm.

I'm Anna. I'm going to be all right.

I'm going to be all right. Breathe. Quietly.
Quietly . . . I was born fifteen years ago . . .

And I hear her voice. Marni speaking the words that used to hypnotise me to sleep when I was little: 'It's two a.m. . . . on a freezing February morning. We're in the car, Dad and I, on the way to hospital. But you're in such a hurry . . .' Her voice smiles. 'And then there you are – in the car . . . eyes wide open, looking up at me, listening. All ready . . . all ready for life.'

6

Bahrain - 13.00 hrs

While Anna is flying towards Beirut to refuel, her two brothers are kicking a football around on the roof of their house in Bahrain. They've made water bombs out of small balloons, collected them in a basket and are waiting to throw them at the taxi driver who pretended to run them down the day before. He always cruises by about now.

They keep looking over the balustrade, but there's no sign of him.

'What about that one?' Mark points at a cyclist wobbling towards them across the wasteland in a trail of dust.

'But...' Sam looks doubtful.

'Oh, come on. He's probably the one who chased Anna.'

When the man is under the parapet, they drop their load. The two water bombs hit the ground, making small wet explosions in the sand by the man's feet. He slews to one side, rights himself, looks up and waves his fist at the two grinning faces before they duck behind the wall and roll on the ground, hooting.

But Marni has seen the cyclist from the sitting-room window and guesses what the boys are up to.

She races upstairs and spots the pile of water bombs. 'What do you think you're doing?' she says crossly. The boys search for a reprieve in her eyes, but find none. 'Obviously I can't trust you to behave up here, so you'd better go and play downstairs.'

The boys trot down in front of her, one holding the football, the other the basket of bombs. 'You'd better give the rest of those to me,' she says. 'You can play in your room until lunch.' She doesn't want anything to spoil their last day together. They'll be back at school in England tomorrow. 'And Mark,' she calls as they disappear down the corridor, 'if you're thinking of playing rough games, put your violin away first.'

She sits sewing the last nametapes onto their uniforms at the dining-room table. She hates them going. She's missing Anna so much already. Missing seeing her sprawled out on the floor, stroking the dog, or spinning into the room dropping everything she's carrying to kiss everyone hello, or climbing into bed in the mornings for a chat.

She folds away the last pair of shorts and thinks of Anna way up in the sky. She hopes she has someone interesting sitting next to her. There were a few other schoolchildren at the airport, one or two Anna's age.

The back door slams. It's James coming back from work for lunch. He puts his cap down on the table and kisses her on the forehead. 'Nearly there,' he says.

'Yes, nearly there.'

'What else needs doing?' He wipes away the sweat on his forehead with the back of his hand.

'Just last-minute packing. Call the boys. Lunch is nearly ready.'

The shrill sound of the phone ringing echoes round the bare room.

James picks up the receiver. 'Hello, James Milton here.'

Marni stands up and starts to pack away her sewing things. She glances up at James, something in his stance stops her. He listens for a while, frowning, then goes still, puts one hand on the table as if for support. 'Yes, sir. I see.'

Something's wrong, something in his voice.

Alarm flutters in her chest.

'What exactly does that mean? Yes. Cancelled. Right. Where to? RAF flight. Yes. Will do. Do you...? Thank you for letting us know.' He puts the phone down, stands looking down at it.

'What?' Marni says. 'What is it?' He turns. 'What?' she cries.

He shakes his head.

'James!'

'Anna,' he says.

'What? For God's sake!'

'Hijacked.'

Marni's hand shoots to her mouth. 'No.' She feels both legs going, reaches out, grips the back of a chair.

They sit opposite each other, uncomprehending.

He puts out his hands, holds hers. 'Palestinians. PFLP. Got on in India, hijacked it before it got to Beirut.'

'Like those others,' she says.

'Yes. They're Palestinian refugees. They've involved the British because of the hijacker being held in London, taken off the El Al plane that was diverted to Heathrow last week.

29

They want her released.'

'Where's Anna now?'

'They think the plane's heading for Beirut.'

'Is she alive?'

He puts his arms around her. 'They don't know. They think so.'

7

Beirut - 13.00 hrs

The hijackers have allowed the crew to hand round drinks. All the adult passengers are knocking back booze like there's no tomorrow. Not us though, or the Arab family opposite. We've all had Cokes or lemonade. And now Rosemary and Celia, the other air hostess, are handing out white plastic trays of cold lunch. The salad is a lettuce with a boiled egg on top and one of those green olives stuffed with a sliver of red. There's a small packet of cream crackers, a hard little glazed roll, a rectangle of butter in silver foil that looks more like a chocolate, and a miniature slab of tough Cheddar cheese in cellophane. The tiny plastic glass and teacup, the miniature salt and pepper shakers and the plastic dishes all fitting together make me feel like I'm oversized and eating a picnic in a doll's house.

Up in first class, they're sipping champagne and choosing from a trolley with warm rolls, fresh cheeses and grapes.

But I don't feel like eating anything anyway. My stomach's churning. David says he's starving, says we should eat because we don't know when the next meal will be. He's almost cleared everything on his tray already.

He looks over at mine. 'Do you really not want it?'

I shake my head. 'Help yourself.'

Tim picks at his dry roll. 'You know the dog you left behind, Anna? What sort was he?'

'Well, I don't know really. A mongrel, I suppose. He's honey-coloured with feathery britches, and he likes chasing cars.'

He looks impressed. 'If you're missing him a lot,' he says, 'I could draw him for you.'

'That's kind! Can you give him flying ears too,' I say.

'OK.' Tim pushes his tray to one side and pulls a red Etch-A-Sketch out of his satchel. He starts twiddling the knobs, making lines on the screen.

'Where d'you live in Bahrain then?' David says, wiping his mouth on his napkin. He's really perked up now, since eating all three of our custardy puddings.

'Near Juffair,' I say. 'Just outside the barracks, in one of the white houses. But actually nowhere, pretty soon.'

'Why?'

'We're not going back. Dad's posting has ended.'

'Shame,' he says.

'Look.' Tim has made an angular doggy outline.

'That's really good,' I say.

'D'you think they will let us get off at Beirut?' Tim asks, shading in Woofa's britches. David and I exchange glances.

But it's Celia, collecting our trays, who answers. 'We're only refuelling at Beirut.' She pushes a stray bit of hair back into her peroxide-blonde bun. 'We won't be getting off, I'm afraid.'

'Well, that settles that,' says David, when she's moved off.

Tim shows me his finished picture of Woofa. It's not bad. He's chasing a car with his ears flying out behind him, but the sight of him makes me feel suddenly intensely homesick.

After the meal everyone starts chain-smoking. Or that's how it feels. The cabin fills with smoke. It hangs in clouds around our heads, thick and suffocating.

Eventually we're told to put our seats upright and our tables away in preparation for landing. There's an air of anticipation in the cabin, but not a healthy, relaxed sort, more a sense of dread.

We've been dropping steeply for a while, and my heart lurches when I hear the clunk of the wheels lowering. Will the government in Beirut let a hijacked plane land and refuel without doing anything to get us out? Surely they'll try and rescue us?

But what if they try and it doesn't work?

'David,' I whisper, turning my head so that Tim can't hear, 'do you think they *will* just let us refuel?'

'God knows,' he says.

'Not try to free us?'

'I'd like to know how,' he says. 'The moment they make a move, we're finished.' I wish I hadn't asked. 'We'll be dead meat,' he adds.

No need to rub it in, I think.

'D'you know what?' he says suddenly. 'It's probably better not to think about it.'

But I can't stop. *What if landing jolts the bomb? Or someone tries to overcome the hijackers and . . . Can you storm a plane with a bomb on board without blowing everyone up?* It feels like blood is frothing in my chest.

We're about to land. I glimpse a green hill and some trees before I'm thrown forward and the plane touches down. It jerks and slows, the engines reverse in a deafening roar, then quieten. We've landed. We taxi along the main runway before turning off onto a smaller one. *We haven't blown up. WE HAVEN'T BLOWN UP!*

Everyone begins to crowd around the windows. I undo my belt and peer out of Tim's porthole. All I can see are a few roads winding uphill, some white houses and smoke rising. As we continue taxiing, through the windows on the other side I can just make out bits of paved runway, a bank of airport lights on red-and-white posts, a patch of scrubland and, far off, a few parked planes and what must be the main airport building. It seems an awfully long way off. There are Jeeps parked outside and a crowd of people milling about, some of them soldiers.

They don't look like they're about to rescue us. They look too disorganised, almost relaxed. Don't they realise what's happening out here?

But then it becomes obvious. We've been put as far away as possible from everything, like we have some contagious disease, because they *know* we might explode at any moment, that we might be blown to pieces here on the ground instead of up in the air.

Nothing much happens for ages. The cabin is unnaturally quiet. The cabin crew are still in their seats. We wait. Only Sweaty and the Giant are up, standing expectantly by the closed front door. What are *they* waiting for?

Through the windows in the other side, I catch a glimpse of some white steps approaching across the runway, looking as though they are driving themselves, but there's a man crouched underneath steering them. Whose side is he on? Is he armed?

Does he realise that if he's not careful, the hijackers will blow us up?

I feel as if my head will burst with it all. Suddenly the light changes at the front of the aircraft. Someone has opened the door. I think about the fresh air curling in and floating down the aisle and I imagine getting up and running out and down the steps... but then what?

There's a brief conversation in Arabic between the hijackers and the man on the steps and the door closes again. We're shut back in.

'Oh, for heaven's sake,' I say.

Tim stares disconsolately out of his window. 'Waiting's *so* boring,' he says. 'Nothing's happening and there's nothing to see.'

'I can see the steps from here,' the Arab man opposite says to us. 'They're on their way back to the main terminal building.'

'Oh,' says David. 'Thanks.'

'And,' the man continues, 'a yellow truck is coming out, probably to refuel.'

We hear various clunks outside the plane. I think of all the liquid fuel pouring into the tanks, how inflammable it is – and I push the thought away.

'There's a man watching the refuelling standing just below, look, there.' Tim points. 'He's just wearing ordinary clothes. I wish he'd look up. I've written a message to him on my Etch-A-Sketch asking him to save us. Look.'

'I'm not sure that's a good idea, Tim. He might be a hijacker,' I say. 'Better rub it out.'

'The steps are coming back,' the man opposite says. After a few moment, he adds, 'A woman and a man are on them this time, standing at the top.'

The door at the front of the plane opens again. We hear the two newcomers climbing aboard and strain to look. To begin with I glimpse only the side of a shoulder. Then the woman steps into view. She glances briefly down the plane at us, and then continues talking to Sweaty and the Giant. She's youngish, in jeans, with a leather bag over her shoulder, and she's wearing a silky silver headscarf and black-rimmed specs that obscure her eyes. Her companion, in dull grey office trousers and a white shirt, comes over and offers her a cigarette. She takes one and he lights it with a gold lighter. The flame blazes up, making her glasses glint. She takes a drag, turns to him, slaps him on the back, seems animated, happy even, as though this is some kind of reunion, some sort of celebration.

'Who do you think *they* are?' David whispers. 'More hijackers?'

'Looks like it.' My heart sinks. Now there's no chance of rescue.

'Just wait till I tell my friends!' Tim says. 'I've been held up at gunpoint, sat near a bomb, that man at the back wanting to go to the toilet nearly got us all shot, and now the plane's filling up with hijackers.' But then his face clouds over. 'They won't believe me, will they?'

'I think they might,' I say. 'It'll probably be on TV.'

I think of Marni, Dad and the boys watching the news, maybe seeing footage of the plane landing in Beirut. What will they think? What will they say? Do they know I'm here? Do they know I'm still alive?

'Are you thirsty?' he asks.

'Yes.'

'Me too.'

'I expect they'll put some more food and drinks on for us soon.' But no food or drinks arrive. Rosemary and Celia continue to accompany passengers up and down to the toilets. There are two at the front and four at the back. Celia is 'doing' our side of the plane. She looks nervy when she isn't flashing her fake smile.

Suddenly a baby begins to cry. It's a tense high-pitched wail, of pain or panic. It sounds shocking at first, and then becomes unbearable. It's recognisable somehow, as though on some level he's doing what we all want to. I turn to try and see the baby. They're a few rows behind us. The mother is asking Celia whether she thinks he's teething or has earache. Celia looks at her as if to say, *How on earth should I know? You're the mother.* But she bends down and peers at the baby.

A tall, pale woman in a gingham dress across the aisle and a little way back calls for help. Her daughter has just been sick all down her front. The smell of it filters down the aisle. We hold our noses, pull our tops over our faces and then giggle hysterically, it's so awful.

Rosemary comes to mop it up with tissues, disinfectant and water. I definitely couldn't do her job. Unfortunately the combination of disinfectant and sick makes the smell worse.

The baby continues to scream, though I think I'm getting used to it now. I can almost block it out. The Giant lumbers down and escorts the mother and baby to a bulkhead seat at the front, where he says there's a carrycot. He still looks as though nothing fazes him, like this hijacking is all in a day's work.

I'm desperate to stretch my legs and trying hard not to think how claustrophobic it is in here. At last Celia beckons to David for his turn to go to the toilet. I'm next!

While he's away from his seat, I watch the Arab family opposite. The man wears an immaculate long white robe, a *thawb*, with crisp ironed creases down the sleeves. His wife is entirely in black. I can't see her face, just the edge of a soft gold bangle as she tends to their little baby son. She has her arm around him while she reads to him. His fat little legs waggle with delight. Seeing her tenderness towards him reminds me of home, and another wave of homesickness washes over me. What I'd do to be with my family, to have their arms round *me*. I'm missing them so badly it hurts. It's not ordinary sad, going-back-to-school sad, but a draggingly deep sorrow that I've never felt before.

David comes back, and at last it's my turn to get up and walk about. I follow Celia, glancing down the plane at all the disembodied heads turning, chatting, smoking. Some stare morosely ahead. An older couple gulp back whisky in unison. Two boys, who look like twins in identical maroon-and-grey school blazers, crouch up on their seats and pass toys over the top to those behind them. The bomber sits dead still, wearing his sinister dark glasses. His suitcase sticks slightly out into the aisle. Those sitting nearest him seem more subdued than the others. Sweaty's standing right at the back holding his gun, a picture of unease.

I move to the front, passing the two girls with blonde hair from the queue at the airport. They are both a bit older than me and wearing floral miniskirts and matching tops. One's plaiting the other one's hair. They look up as I go by and I feel their eyes on my back. I pass the baby crying in the carrycot, his face screwed up in outrage, pink and gasping. His mother strokes his head, looking glazed, as if she's completely given up trying to quieten him.

I walk past the two new hijackers sitting at the front in first class, deep in conversation and eating lunch from airline trays. Then I squeeze past the Giant at the front with his gun trained on the cabin.

Reaching the toilet, I close the door on them all, and lock it. In the mirror, under the strip lighting, I'm shocked to be confronted by this tired girl with worried grey eyes and mussed-up hair. I stare at her. She seems different; older, careworn.

I try combing my hair with my fingers, but soon give up. It's too tangled to make much difference. How stupid not to bring a hairbrush. I splash water on my face and dry it on the paper towels. And it feels really good. I use the toilet, wash my hands and my armpits with soap and water and dry them too. I think about scooping up some of the water, but it says 'not drinking water' so I don't risk it. It's such a relief to be alone, though even in here I can still hear the baby's plaintive cries. I wonder how long I can stay without Celia badgering me. I try stretching out my arms and jiggling my feet about as though I'm warming up for a diving competition. It's too cramped, but it's my space, just for this moment, and I like it.

What if something happens though? What if I hear shots or someone tries to overpower the hijackers? What if everyone's rescued but me?

My face looks terrible.

Help me then, I say to the girl in the glass.

She stares back. Mute.

Marni would say, *Anna, I think you need to have a good cry.* She says crying's good for you. Bottling things up isn't.

The girl in the mirror's definitely bottled up.

Cry then, I say to her. But her face is set in stone, her eyes hard and dark and haunted.

You have no feeling, I say. And it's true. I feel numb, empty.

Suddenly there's a brisk *rat-a-tat-tat* on the door. 'Hello? Time to finish up.' Celia's impatient.

Finish up. Finish up where? Good question, I say to the reflection in the glass. Then I unlatch the door.

On my way back down the aisle, I notice that the girl with red-blonde hair in first class has moved to sit beside the bald cigar-smoking man. He's complaining in a loud voice to the steward about not being offered a *double* gin '*in the circumstances.*'

I squeeze past Rosemary, tending to the baby. He's really letting rip now, his lungs fit to burst. His mother stands by helplessly, looking even more wrung out. Rosemary's pouring some liquid painkiller into his bottle.

After Tim's been to the toilet and we're all back sitting down, Rosemary brings round a tray full of small plastic glasses of water, one for each of us. Before I can stop him, Tim tops Fred's water up with his.

'Tim! *You* need that!' I cry.

'But... it's just... I was worried...' His face crumples.

'You're probably right,' I say quickly. 'Fred needed more too. Here, have some of mine.'

With Sweaty at the back, the Giant at the front, the bomber in the middle and the two new hijackers sitting in first class, the plane takes off again. I glance at my watch. 2.30. There's that moment of weightlessness and then the lurch as my stomach hits the ceiling.

I look through Tim's window at the hazy shapes below getting smaller and smaller. The plane circles over the airport, stops climbing so steeply and levels out.

'We're not going so high,' I say.

'No.' David's face is resigned. 'Looks like they really are taking us to their Revolutionary Airstrip after all.'

'And I was hoping for a miracle,' I say.

'Well –' Tim leans forward to looks at us – 'we're still all in one piece.' David and I smile at each other, surprised, then look back at him. 'What?' he says, frowning. 'It's what my dad says.'

'And it's perfect,' I say. He looks pleased.

At last the baby's cries gradually begin to subside into sobs, then snuffles, then silence as he sleeps. And the plane continues droning on and on in the wrong direction.

8

15.30 hrs

The captain has just come onto the intercom to tell us that we're still flying south from Beirut, down the Mediterranean coast. Tim and I look out of the window, but there's nothing but sea on this side.

'What about a game of cards, you two?' David slaps a pack down on my table. 'Can you play whist?' He starts to shuffle, slicing the cards around, arcing and flipping them together, looking worryingly expert.

He explains the rules to us, and then deals. I look at my hand, trying to remember what he's just said, but I can't focus properly. My brain just hasn't taken it in.

David starts winning one trick after another.

'You've played this a lot, haven't you?' I say.

'Yep.' He grins and trumps me again. When he wins the game, he shuffles and deals once more.

I look at my new cards. 'David, you can't have shuffled them properly.'

'What's the matter? Bad hand?'

'Yes. *Again.*'

His tricks pile up.

Tim looks despondent. 'I've only managed to win one trick!'

'It's because *he* keeps changing the rules,' I say, leaning the other way, trying to steal a look at David's cards.

'Hey!' He moves them out into the aisle where I can't see. 'Typical!'

'Typical cheat,' I say, putting down a feeble two of clubs. 'We'll play cheat next, Tim. Then we can *all* do it.'

'Would this be because I'm winning?' David asks airily. And then when he does win: 'I don't expect you want another game?'

I shake my head. 'No, thanks.'

While David gathers up the cards and packs them away, Tim gets his Etch-A-Sketch out again.

'I'm going to draw you, Anna, and then you, David,' he says.

And soon the wobbly lines of an unflattering portrait appear on the screen. 'Really!' I cry. 'Look at the size of my nose!'

'Sorry.' Tim tips the Etch-A-Sketch up to clear the screen and starts again.

'What about that?' he says.

'Much better. Though my chin's a bit on the witchy side.'

David leans over to look. 'No, I'd say that's quite accurate.'

Suddenly the intercom crackles overhead and we all tense.

'*...do you mean?*' The captain's voice is full of anger. '*Look, if you can't give me better co-ordinates than that, we'll never find it! We've been going up and down searching for your bloody*

Revolutionary Airstrip for nearly an hour now. There's a bloody big piece of desert down there and a lot of sea, and we're running out of fuel. You've got to give me a more accurate positioning!'
We hear another voice in the background, then the captain shouts, '*I don't care! I have the safety of my passengers to consider, never mind landing this aircraft in the middle of the bloody desert. Now, get me better co-ordinates, before we run out of fuel and come down anyway.'*

Come down anyway. The terrible words sink in.

David avoids meeting my eye. Tim looks fixedly out of the window. I can't take much more of this. I think of the fuel burning up, the plane's tanks getting emptier and emptier as we carry on, going nowhere. I stare down at my tray lying neatly folded in two, the metal ring for the drink I do not have lying uppermost. We played cards on this tray. No one's playing now. Nothing's funny any more.

It seems like an eternity before the captain comes back on the intercom, officially this time, to announce that the crew have located the Revolutionary Airstrip, and that he is going to attempt a landing. The hijackers, he says, have assured him that the ground is in good condition.

'I hope he knows what he's doing,' David mutters.

9

16.45 hrs

The two air hostesses come through the cabin to make sure that cigarettes are extinguished, seatbelts fastened, chairbacks upright and trays put away. They also spend time reassuring us that we'll make it down safely, but then they ask us to look at the brace position on the cards in our seat pockets in case of an emergency landing.

On her way back up to the front, Rosemary stops to talk to the two blonde girls. 'It'll be OK,' I hear her say. 'Really. They've assured the captain that it is possible to land a VC10 there.'

'But it's desert,' the older one, in the outside seat, says. Rosemary crouches down, puts her arm around her and talks quietly and intently for a minute. Then Celia comes and nods towards the front. It's time for them to be seated.

Are these my last moments on earth? I feel an overpowering disbelief. They can't be. This can't be it. Was that all? My life. Was that it? What was the last thing I said to Marni? Why didn't I hug Dad longer? Will the boys forget about me as they get older? My heart is thumping so loudly that I move my arm away from David in case he can feel it.

Tim has gone very quiet. He's looking out of the window, clasping Fred's tin tightly on his lap.

'Tim, do you think maybe you should put Fred down on the floor? He might be safer there when we land. You could even wedge the tin between your feet.'

'All right.' I can see he's reluctant to let go of him.

'He'll be better down there. Honestly.'

The plane starts to descend very steeply and the baby in the carrycot starts screaming again. Rosemary gets up and passes the mother, Sarah, a beaker. The water sloshing inside the pale blue plastic reminds me again how thirsty I am.

I hear the wing flaps moving out and down ready for landing. The baby's cries subside. There's an eerie hush in the cabin as the wheels lower. I peer out of Tim's window. Sand the colour of pale tea stretches to the horizon. Can you really land a huge heavy plane on sand?

Down, down we go.

I close my eyes, willing the captain to land safely. Praying we will make it. *Go on! You can do it.*

Come on! Come on!

No one speaks. We're all desperately praying for a safe landing. I hold my breath, waiting for the impact.

Down, down, closer and closer. We coast in mid-air, then...crunch! The back wheels hit the ground, the nose lowers and the plane jolts violently as the front wheel touches down. The engines reverse in a blasting roar, and the great body of the plane shudders and shakes under the stress. Huge clouds of red sand roll up on either side of the cabin, obscuring the view. We're level but bumping, lurching and sliding, braking and slowing some more, taxiing in a storm of red sand. I lean forward and stare out of the window, waiting for the dust to disperse. It's another world.

We career along, slowing little by little, and gradually shapes begin to appear though the billowing red clouds: the wheel of a Jeep, a leg hanging down, the muzzle of a gun, a scarfed head. And as the sand thins, I see a row of Jeeps with machine guns mounted on them travelling alongside us at exactly the same speed we're moving. The Jeeps are covered in people, hanging off the sides, holding onto the canopy, sitting on the bonnet, standing at the back – all waving guns over their heads, laughing, cheering, men, women and teenagers, some in khaki, others in camouflage gear. All of them wear black berets or keffiyeh, black-and-white checked scarves to protect them from the dust, and all eyes are on the plane. I feel as if I'm in some kind of dream. And, for a brief, peculiar moment, that I'm the only person on this plane. That they are all looking only at me.

And I can't believe we landed without crashing.

A sense of uneasy relief sweeps through the cabin. A safe landing, but what's next? What about the armed guerrillas outside?

We taxi to a halt. The Giant, Sweaty and the steward go to open the door nearest to the cockpit. I hear shouts – *Al ham du lilla*, thank God. *Ahlan wasaklan*, welcome – and instructions in Arabic that I don't understand. All the energy and excitement feels odd when we sit here in rows, in shock, like sitting ducks.

Tim picks up Fred's tin and opens it.

'Look, Anna.' He's smiling. 'He's all right!'

I peer in. 'He even looks like he enjoyed the landing.'

'*Ladies and gentlemen and children,*' the captain says over the intercom. '*Well, that was interesting – but we did it!*' The relief in his voice makes him sound younger. '*You can now undo your seatbelts, but please remain seated – just for a little longer, until we have talked to the hijackers on the ground. Thank you very much.*'

Rosemary seems to be helping to open the door nearest the cockpit.

'Hold on, Alan,' I hear her call to the chief steward. 'I think they want us to undo the emergency rope, so they can fix it to that wooden ladder. They're shouting up for it.'

'OK, here it comes. Tie it to that Jeep,' Alan shouts down.

Once the rope and wooden ladder are in place, more guerrillas pour on board. They take it in turns to look down the aisle at us, at their *captives*, and their faces register a kind of astonishment, then pride and delight. Two new ones walk down and station themselves at the back of the plane.

There's a disturbance behind me. I crane my neck to see. The man with the bomb briefcase is slowly walking up the aisle towards us, still wearing his sunglasses. His steps are measured, deliberate. When he passes by, the passengers lean slightly away from him, as though he's contaminated. And as he gets closer to me, I see that the briefcase is on a long chain handcuffed to his wrist. He has dark stubble on his wide creased face and his mouth turns up at the edges in a permanent half-smile. His small ears stand out like molluscs from his shaven head. I can smell his acidic aftershave long after he's gone.

When he reaches the front, he immediately disappears into the cockpit. The captain, his two co-pilots and the navigator are quickly ejected and the door is closed firmly behind them.

They stand displaced, out of context, at the front of the plane. The captain's jaw is set, his mouth grim. He has thick white hair, a long face and an authoritative air. He stands tall and dignified, his arms loose at his sides.

'I cannot agree to turning off the engines,' he says to the two hijackers who boarded at Beirut. 'If I do, there'll be no air conditioning or pumps for water and the toilets will fail.'

But the hijackers insist. 'If the engines aren't shut down,' the woman says clearly in good English, 'you might try to escape.'

'Get this thing in the air without you noticing?' the captain says. 'Nonsense! You do know that once the power's off, you can't start it up again.' He looks in frustration at the navigator, who shakes his head in disbelief.

'You'll really regret it,' the navigator says in a Scottish accent. 'How the hell are you going to look after all these people without toilets or water? Without air conditioning, in these temperatures?'

But the hijackers won't budge. In fact, they force the two men back into the cockpit, to switch everything off. The co-pilots are told to sit down in the empty first-class seats at the front.

Suddenly all the neon lights in the ceiling recesses over the aisle go off, all the no-smoking signs disappear and the air con shuts down. The little hose sending out a wonderful stream of cold air above my head stops. I put my hand up to check. Nothing. I try the light switch. Dead.

As the cool cabin air escapes into the desert, and the intense heat of the desert swirls in, the temperature begins to rise.

I lean my head against the once-cool plastic of the seat in front. It's warm and sticky already.

With the no-smoking signs unlit, cigarette lighters start clicking all round the cabin, and smoke curls above the seats around us. Soon cigarette smoke is all I can smell. And as it gets hotter and hotter, the cabin appears to shrink into the fug.

10

Revolutionary Airstrip, Jordan - 17.20 hrs

Apart from the occasional low voice and the rustle of hot, restless, cooped-up bodies, it's unnaturally quiet now. There's no noise from the plane's engine, no air conditioning and no intercom any more.

We sit quietly, sweltering under the great blanket of heat weighing us down. I've piled my hair up and stuck a pencil in it to keep it off my neck, but it still feels stifling, like I'm wearing a thick woollen hat. The straggly bits stick to the sweat on my face and neck. Everything is sticking. My clothes are stuck to my body. My shirt is stuck to my back. My skirt is stuck to my legs, which are stuck to the seat. I'm stuck here, sweating endlessly, and there's nothing I can do about it. And everything is an effort. Lifting my arm, turning my head, bending down, I do it all in slow motion.

I wonder if thinking about cool things will help. Like the first time I visited London from abroad when it was winter and freezing cold and raining. We all sat in a cafe watching the people walk to work holding briefcases and umbrellas, and we wondered what was the matter with them. Why were they all walking *so fast*? What had happened? Were they running away from something? Because no one walked *that* fast in the hot country we lived in then. They're walking fast to keep warm, Marni had said. Everyone slows down in the heat, to keep cool.

I wish there was some *cool* in here.

I take my shoes off, blow down my front, wave magazines around to try to stir up the air, to create just the tiniest of breezes, but it's hopeless. Then I remember the BOAC paper fan stuffed down in my seat pocket. I pull it out and whip it to and fro, but I'm just moving hot air around. I give up, defeated.

'This is unbearable,' I grumble.

'And it's only going to get worse.' David wipes a rivulet of sweat from his neck with a tissue.

'Well, thanks, David,' I say. 'Guaranteed to raise spirits.'

He laughs shortly. 'Sorry. Didn't realise that was my designated role.'

'It won't be this hot when it gets dark, will it?' Tim says hopefully, his face bright pink.

'No, it should cool down,' David says, 'but then we'll probably freeze. We're in the desert, after all.'

'Great,' I say. 'Though frankly anything will be better than this. Even the soles of my feet are sweating, for God's sake.'

'If I was in a cartoon,' Tim says, 'there'd be smoke coming out of my ears.'

'Why don't you roll up the sleeves of your shirt? And I'd take your shoes and socks off too.' I help get him organised.

'Funny we haven't heard about the other planes,' David says. 'They must be here too somewhere.'

'The two hijacked earlier? Why don't you ask him?' I nod at the Arab opposite.

'Good idea.' David leans over and touches him on the arm. 'Excuse me, sir,' he says. 'We heard that two other planes were hijacked and taken to Jordan earlier this week and we wondered if you can see them through your window. There aren't any on this side.'

'Yes, yes, dear boy,' he replies kindly. 'Apparently they are here, but it's difficult to see through these portholes. The Swissair is further back and on our left – I can *just* see the nose – and the air hostess said the TWA was behind us, so out of sight. But mostly I only see guerrillas swarming about.'

'Thanks.' David turns back to us. 'Did you get that?' Tim and I nod. 'I wonder what the people in those planes are feeling like by now? They've been here three days already. Christ, I couldn't take this heat for three days.'

'Do you think they have bombs on board too?' Tim asks.

'I expect so,' replies David.

'They must have given them some food,' Tim says, 'or they'd be skeletons by now.'

'No, not quite yet, Tim,' David says. 'And of course they'll be feeding them.' But I can see he's not so sure.

'Do you think someone there will seriously lose it, like that man at the back did?' Tim asks cheerfully.

'You mean they'll be shooting?' David says. 'And because we're close enough, we blow up as well?'

'Er, thanks, you two, that's probably enough.' They're making me feel jittery again.

David puts an arm around me. 'We'd better stop, Tim.' He shakes his head. '*She* can't take it.'

I shrug him off. 'God, you're so patronising. Why don't we swap seats, so you two boys can talk fascinating boys' stuff together, and I can sit in peace in the aisle seat for a change?'

David raises his eyebrows. 'You really want to?'

'Yes, just for a bit.'

'OK.' He lifts the armrest and I semi-stand while he slides under me into my seat, and I try slipping into his. It's a bit of a sticky tangle, and at one point I regret asking him, but we do manage it – eventually.

I'm just settling down to enjoy the new, clear view up and down the aisle, when my calm is broken by the captain raising his voice at the front: 'But the passengers haven't had anything proper to eat or drink for ages,' he says to the Giant. 'We didn't take on any supplies at Beirut except fuel, so we'll need food and water to be brought on board very soon.'

'I'm sorry,' the Giant replies. 'But we have none spare at the moment. You will have to wait.'

I turn to David. 'Did you hear that?'

'He can't be serious,' he says.

'Where have the other two hijackers gone?' the captain asks. 'The ones that got on at Beirut. I need to speak to them urgently.'

'I'm sorry, they are busy on the ground. There is nothing I can do at the moment.' The Giant's voice is deep and patient. The captain gives him a frosty look and sits back down across the aisle from the navigator.

I sit quietly while the boys play interminable games of hangman, then noughts and crosses. After that, David tries to draw Sweaty in Tim's school uniform on his Etch-A-Sketch.

'Where's your school then, Tim?' he asks as he draws.

'In Kent. I don't like it much. The older boys are bullies. You have to do things for them *all* the time. One of the assistant matrons is nice though.'

'What's her name?' David is turning Sweaty into a rat with bulging eyes and drooling gums.

'She's called Miss Thomas. She lets me play with her Jack Russell, Dandy. She'll like Fred. I know she will.'

David rubs Sweaty out, and puts down the Etch-A-Sketch. 'No offence to you two, but I'm feeling *really* tired of sitting here. I need to get up and *walk*.'

'Go on then,' I say. 'Give it a try. We'll watch. See if you get shot.'

He looks sideways at me and screws up his face. 'You'd like that, wouldn't you?'

I shrug. 'Wouldn't mind.'

'Charming.'

'Why don't you draw the Giant now?'

'Screen's too small.'

'Do you want your seat back then?' I ask.

'OK.'

While I'm settling back down next to Tim, he suddenly asks whether I have a brother.

'Yes,' I say. 'Two. Why?'

'I've always wanted one,' he says. 'How old are yours?'

'They're eleven and nine.'

'I'm nine too.' Tim looks pleased. 'And do you have a father *and* a mother?'

'Yes...' I frown. 'Why?'

'Oh, well, I don't.' He says it matter-of-factly.

'I'm sorry,' I say quietly. 'Your mother?'

'Yes.' He looks straight at me with serious brown eyes. 'She died when I was six.'

'Oh, Tim. That's so sad.'

'She was called Anna too, you know. We have pictures of her, lots of them, all over the house. Dad still loves her, you see. If she was alive I wouldn't be here. I wouldn't go to boarding school. Sometimes I dream about her. I'm sure it's her.'

'Who looks after you when you're home, when your dad's at work?'

'Our housekeeper, Mary. She stayed ever since Mum died. I write to her when I'm at school – as well as Dad.'

'What does your dad do?'

'He's an engineer.'

'What's yours?' David asks me.

'In the army. Mum's a teacher.'

'Ah! There she is,' Rosemary says from the aisle. 'Just the girl I want.' Sweaty's standing behind her so I feel a shock of anxiety. 'Don't look so worried!' Rosemary says. 'I'm just wondering if you'd like to help me go through the trays at the back in the galley to find any uneaten food left over from lunch? Fancy it?'

I look at Sweaty; his gun is pointing at the ground for once. I'd *really* like to get up and walk about. I nod. 'Thanks.' I begin to climb past David, but he springs up to let me out.

'How come she's been hand-picked?' he asks Rosemary.

She laughs. 'Hand-picked? You'll get your turn, don't worry.'

When he's back in his seat, I lean down. 'You see, David,' I whisper, 'there are some advantages in being a girl!'

I follow Rosemary to the back of the plane.

'Now,' she says when we get to the galley, 'I'm Rosemary.' She points to her badge. 'And you're...?'

'Anna.'

'Good, lovely.' She has lively brown eyes and short curly hair the colour of conkers. I can't get over how brave she was with the hijackers when that man wanted to go to the toilet. Would I do that? I doubt it.

'We need to go through all these used trays in the trolleys,' she explains, 'and pick out any wrapped food that's left. Only unopened stuff, mind you. Excuse me,' she says a little sharply to Sweaty who's in the way. He moves to one side and she kneels down and slides out the top tray from one of the metal cabinets. 'Crackers, cheese, cans of drink and water, especially water. Remember, leave anything that's been opened. Isn't it crazy?' she says. 'We've got masses of duty-free booze, cigarettes, perfume, but hardly any food or water. They might have thought that one through in Beirut.' She picks up a sealed pack of crackers. 'Pile it up on here, and we'll share it all out later. Why don't you start on this trolley?' She points to the one nearest the aisle.

I start sliding the trays out one by one and sifting through them. Loads of people have only taken one bite or spoonful and then left the rest, not able to eat then, like me, I suppose. They must be regretting it now. I certainly am. What I'd do to be offered that tray full of food again.

Though I'm uncomfortable having Sweaty's gun trained on my back, it's good to be somewhere else, doing something different, bending and stretching, not having to think about missing Marni or Tim's sad story or being blown up.

Suddenly the chief steward, Alan, steps past Sweaty and into the galley.

'Oh, hello,' Rosemary says with a quick smile. 'This is Anna.'

'How're you doing?' Alan says to me. He's probably thirty-something, but looks older, worn out – as worn as Rosemary looks fresh.

'I'm OK, thanks,' I say, pushing a tray in and pulling out another.

'What brings you down here?' Rosemary asks him.

'Well, as you know,' he says airily, 'I just can't leave you alone.' Rosemary shares a long-suffering look with me. 'Actually,' he says, 'I thought you might like a hand.' He starts rolling up his shirtsleeves and I find myself wishing he hadn't come. Being with just Rosemary felt much less complicated.

'Celia and I have finished going through the food cabinets at the front,' Alan says, dropping a small tin of tonic on the counter. 'Not much there, I'm afraid. Why we didn't take on meals in Beirut I'll never understand.'

'Well, let's hope we have more luck here,' Rosemary adds a tiny tin of tomato juice to the meagre collection. 'Anna sits between the two boys in Row 10, by the way.'

'Do you now?' Alan grins at me. There's a dark edge to his smile where some of his side teeth are missing. I carry on searching through the trays. He comes and kneels by me. 'Yeah, we only found a few crackers at the front.' His face close up is clammy and pockmarked. 'Oh, and some peaches and about eight bread rolls.'

Rosemary sighs. 'That's not a lot, is it? We've got ninety-eight passengers and seven crew to feed. Oh well, we'll just have to cut them up and share them out as best we can.'

Alan wipes the back of his hand across his forehead. 'They say they might be able to get us some tomatoes and grapes and more water by tomorrow. Just hope they mean it. We'll be pretty desperate by then. I've explained that we have passengers with low-blood-sugar problems, diabetics and the like, who need regular food. Doesn't seem to register though.'

I take a surreptitious look back at Sweaty. His eyes range restlessly up and down the cabin, then back to us. I turn quickly and concentrate on the trays.

'Ta-da!' Rosemary pulls out an intact tin of pineapple juice.

'You know that couple with the pocket radio, the Newtons?' Alan says. 'They say our hijacking was on the last news. Apparently the PFLP have roadblocks in some parts of the capital, Amman, and the King of Jordan's sending tanks in to surround the hijackers. So it's all hotting up, with us in the middle. Even the Syrians are massing troops on the border...' Rosemary shoots Alan a look over my head, stopping him in his tracks. But it's too late, I've heard too much, and it doesn't sound good – *with us in the middle.*

'I've been through the duty-free, by the way,' Alan says. 'Got plenty of booze and a few sodas, loads of gold-plated Dunhill lighters, Nina Ricci scarves, Pierre Cardin stockings, Cognac, miniatures, Peter Stuyvesant and Gitanes cigarettes – but no water or food! Ironic, isn't it? Perhaps we can bribe the hijackers to swap our duty-free for some bread and cheese.'

We've reached the end of the trays and we stand to survey the small heap of food and drinks.

'Thanks, Anna, you've been a real help.' Rosemary smiles. She picks out a packet of crackers and a tiny can of pineapple juice. 'Share that with your two boys. I'll dole this little lot out to everyone else.'

With Alan behind me, I follow Rosemary back up the aisle, carrying my precious hoard. She stops briefly by the little girl who was sick. There's still a whiff of disinfectant around her.

'How are you, Susan? Mrs Green? Everything all right now?' Rosemary asks.

'Yes, thank you.' Mrs Green smiles wanly.

Rosemary looks at Susan, whose mother has taken off her messed-up dress so she is sitting in her knickers. 'You're looking so much better now, Susan. And I hear you're very good at drawing. Have you tried the colouring book yet?' Susan drops her head shyly. Mrs Green smiles gratefully up at Rosemary.

We walk past the couple who were drinking whisky. The man's deep in a *Reader's Digest.* His wife glances up at us from her crossword as we go by. We pass the place where the man with the bomb sat, and then, several rows behind our seats, I'm astonished to see Tim playing Travel Scrabble with the two boys in maroon-and-grey school uniforms. He must have sneaked out while Sweaty's back was turned.

'Got some goodies,' I whisper at him. His eyes light up. He makes quick excuses, slips out and walks in front of me back to our seats. The Arab family opposite David are talking quietly while their son sleeps between them. The couple behind are holding hands, resting with their eyes closed and heads touching.

I sit and put the snack down on my table.

'Hey!' David looks impressed.

'We'll have to take it in turns,' I say. 'Just small sips. No glugging allowed.' I break the can open and take the first tiny sip. The pineapple taste explodes in my mouth. It's unbelievably sweet and so pineapple-y. I pass it on, trying to savour the taste before it goes. But all I want is more.

David takes a sip. 'Ah! Nectar,' he groans.

Tim can't stop grinning. I give them each a cracker.

'Let's see how long we can make them last,' Tim says.

'But I'm salivating already.' David puts the cracker to his nose and inhales it. Then he bites into it quickly. Tim laughs, takes tiny nibbles across it, fast, like a frantic mouse. I eat mine very, very slowly, but even so, it's soon gone, leaving behind only a delicious creamy memory.

11

17.40 hrs

The captain, the navigator, Celia and Rosemary seem to be negotiating with the Giant and Sweaty at the front. The little boy across the aisle has woken up and is driving a Dinky car, a lime-green VW Beetle, up and down his mother's arm and over and back across her table. His father reads a magazine, undisturbed.

'D'you know what?' Tim says. 'The boys further back have got a set of Monopoly!'

'Really?'

'Yes.' He's grinning. 'And loads of other stuff. Walkie-talkies, a Spirograph...'

'Have you told them about Fred?'

'Not yet.' He opens David's pack of cards and starts setting them out for a game of Patience.

David looks at his watch. 'Do you realise, it's past five thirty. Surely they'll let us out soon?'

'Fancy a walk in the desert, do you?' I say.

'Well, anything would be better than this.' He wrenches open his paperback, sighs dramatically and starts to read.

I'm bored too, though I don't want to admit it. How can I possibly feel bored when these might be my last few hours on earth? But I do. And restless. I turn round, kneel on my seat and look back down the plane. The Arab couple opposite glance up briefly, then carry on whispering. I look at the rows and rows of heads: smooth, tufty, ruffled, bald, at the long row of portholes, the only source of light now, and at the endless stretch of overhead shelving rushing towards the back where the toilets and the galley cluster in the dark.

The couple drinking whisky together earlier, that Alan calls 'The Newtons', have swapped places. He's got a small radio pressed up against his ear. Her dyed-blonde bouffant hair now looks like a tousled bird's nest. She's talking across the aisle to an elderly Asian couple.

In front, in first class, Alan, the steward, has twisted round to flirt with the two blonde sisters in miniskirts. He's leaning over offering them a cigarette.

Suddenly the captain peels off from the Giant and the air hostesses and positions himself at the top of the aisle. He raises one hand and calls: 'Ladies and gentlemen, girls and boys...' He pauses until the cabin's quiet. 'The hijackers say that you can now move about a little, not all at once, please, and only quietly and sensibly, for just a few minutes each. So please stretch your legs, have a walk up and down the aisle and then return to your seat. If we can do this without causing the hijackers concern, without too many people doing it at the same time, then I think we may be more comfortable, so please be thoughtful and don't overdo it.'

I stand quickly, slip past David before he can say anything

and walk to the front. I want to get to the open door, to see something else instead of the inside of this plane, to breathe some fresh air.

Alan is standing in the aisle now, still chatting to the girls. I squeeze past him. He smiles and says hi. The two girls completely ignore me. I'm obviously too young to bother about.

I pass the captain, who is standing with the navigator talking with Celia and Rosemary. The Giant stands off to one side, leaning up against the bulkhead, his arms crossed, looking almost relaxed. His gun hangs over his shoulder, the barrel pointing down.

And suddenly I feel exposed being up here alone, but I'm desperate for that fresh air; I feel so sticky and hot. I'm glad there's no sign of Sweaty, and that the cockpit door is firmly closed. Is the man with the bomb still in there? And, if so, what he's doing? I haven't seen him leave. What would I do if he suddenly came out? The thought chills me.

I feel the blast of hot desert air long before I reach the door and have to shield my eyes against the blinding pool of sunlight on the floor, which I pad through in bare feet.

A black crew seat is on the left and folded down, inviting me to sit on it. It's where the crew sit for takeoffs and landings and is held in place by two thick belts attached to the wall.

I put my hand out and touch the heavy metal door. It's inches thick, and has been swung back to the left to lie along the body of the plane. Huge blunt metal teeth down the edge of the doorway fix to the opposing ratchets on the door itself, and there's a great curved metal hinge. No wonder it takes so many people to heave it open. It feels indestructible under my hand, but I don't doubt that if the explosives detonated, the blast would shred this door. And I can't help imagining what it would do to my soft flesh . . .

Ahead of me, a sea of sand stretches away to the horizon, like so many folds in an endless bedsheet. And three tiny horsetail clouds, like delicate brushstrokes, hang high up in the blue.

Across the middle of the open doorway falls a thick rope. It comes out of the wall above the door space where it says: *Escape Rope Behind Flap* and *Emergency Exit*. The rope falls all the way down to the ground, a long way below. If I fell, it would be like falling from a second-storey window – or a high-diving board.

I imagine myself on the high-diving board in Bahrain, opening my arms, flying up and out, that fantastic feeling when you're spreadeagled in mid-air, when, just for a millisecond, the world stands still. Then I'd drop through the air, down, down, until my hands break the water open. And after the impact, I'd also fly but underwater, with my eyes wide open, my arms free in acres of cool water.

Suddenly the rope jerks. I lean out a little and see the shiny black top of Sweaty's head. He's retying it to the bed of the truck below, his gun lying to one side. On the ground is a small round rock, shaped like a resting sheep, and next to it a tough low shrub with one tiny yellow flower.

Through the crack in the door above the curved hinge I can see the cluster of the plane's four back wheels under the wing. And there, a way off, shimmering and distorted by the heat haze, I see the foreshortened shape of the Swissair plane, the red-and-white bulk of it looking preposterous out there in the desert. The windows mirror the sunlight and there aren't any doors open on this side, but I can just make out what look like the wheels of a truck on the other side, under its belly. The idea that some of the passengers shut in there might be able to see our plane feels weird, strange, muddling somehow. I can't see the third plane, the one the man said was directly behind us. I look down again. Sweaty's still busy. I don't want him to see me, so I pull my head back in and stay just inside the doorway.

I stand staring into the open space ahead, at the seemingly endless desert and the low line of far-off hills. And, in the relentless dry heat, with sweat dripping down my back, I dream of fat English clouds heavy with rain, of cool drizzle and mist, of catching the droplets in my mouth. And I think of the huge expanses of cold water covering the earth, and of the days I've spent swimming in the bulging cool of the sea. I think of the boys ducking underwater, doing handstands, the V of their legs wobbling and collapsing, and of them bombing me from the raft tethered inside the shark net, where shoals of tiny fish hide.

Suddenly there's a noise below. I peer over.

Sweaty, his gun slung over one shoulder, is scrambling up the wooden ladder towards me. 'You! You! Go back!' he shouts. I duck back in, adrenaline surging. But he's already in the plane, pushing me. My back slams against the bulkhead. He shoves his face up against mine. My heart's pounding as I blink back tears, smell rancid sweat, his sour breath. And I hate him. For bullying me, for touching me.

Furiously I turn on my heel. But one of the new guards is waiting to leave after his shift. He's standing where the cabin narrows, watching us with intense eyes, his belt crammed with bullets and hung with hand grenades.

I slide back along the galley wall and try to squeeze behind him. But my buckle catches on the back of his belt. I reach quickly to unhitch it, and Sweaty yells, rushes at me, pushes me to one side and grips my arm. I feel the cold muzzle of his gun against my neck and shut my eyes.

Oh God. Oh God.

The muzzle presses deeper. My blood runs like ice in my veins. A wave of nausea, terrifying fear.

Please. Don't!

I can't breathe. My heart's exploding.

'Now, now. Calm down.' It's the Scottish navigator. 'What's the problem here?'

Help me, I plead silently.

'She.' Sweaty shifts the gun until it lies along my jaw. 'She take his ammo,' he spits it out. Flecks land on my neck.

'Nonsense.' The navigator looks at me.

Help me!

'I'm Jim,' he says. 'What happened?'

Can't speak. Can't move. The gun.

Gently Jim pushes the muzzle of Sweaty's gun to one side, puts one arm around me and takes a step away from Sweaty. 'Take a breath.' My legs crumple beneath me. My vision darkens. I can feel the navigator struggling to hold me upright. A sob rises, rips through me. I'm shuddering, gasping for air.

'I...was...get...past...' I start to shake uncontrollably. My knees, my legs, my hands, my arms.

I can't see. Can't hear. My mind's shutting down.

I'm...going...

The navigator's voice is muffled, distorted. 'She was just trying to get past...caught on him...didn't mean to.' Then louder: 'It was a *mistake*.'

I feel a wave of gratitude. Sweaty swims in front of me through the blur, looking unsure. He shrugs, waves us away. The young guard in the ammo belt looks shaken, confused, as I stumble past.

Jim half carries me back down the aisle. He slides me in beside David and pulls my table down. I drop my head onto my folded arms and close my eyes.

'OK?' Jim asks from the aisle.

I nod into the table, still desperately trying to control the shaking.

'You sure?'

I look up briefly. Nod. 'Thanks.' I feel sick, light-headed.

'Look after this wee one for a bit, will you?' he says to David.

'Yes. Sure.'

When Jim's gone, David touches my shoulder. 'Jesus, what happened?'

I shake my head. Can't make words yet. He strokes my back. It feels nice, comforting. After a minute I begin to mumble, 'My buckle...got caught. On the guard's belt.' I pause and take a deep breath. 'On a hand grenade.'

I sit up slowly, clench my fists tight to stop my hands shaking.

'Christ, Anna!' David stares at me, speechless.

I'm overwhelmed with tiredness. I want to go to sleep. I put my head down again.

'Was that why Sweaty was yelling?' he says.

'He thought I was trying to steal it.'

'But you could have been shot!'

I lift my head and look sideways at him, then drop it again.

'God, I hope they get us out of here soon.' David says. 'This is shit.'

12

18.00 hrs

I don't ever want to move again. I sit listening to my ragged breathing, with David quietly beside me.

My heart slowly returns to normal. *Normal.* What's normal? Is this normal now?

Gradually I stop shaking and sit up. I feel weak, like I've been in bed with 'flu for a fortnight.

David's watching me.

'Where's Tim?' I ask.

'Playing Monopoly. It's good he hasn't seen you like this. While you were away he came back specially to tell me that he'd caught the twins passing hotels under the table to each other.'

I smile weakly at him.

'Did you hear that anyone with an Arab, Asian or Indian passport is being allowed to leave the plane?' he asks. 'Apparently the Giant gave the captain a list of about twenty passengers. If they do leave, there'll be less than seventy of us left.' He lowers his voice. 'Our Arab family are going.'

I feel a sharp wave of disappointment. I felt protected somehow by them being there. I look over and realise that the woman is weeping softly – with relief, I suppose. The man comforts her.

He looks over, smiles, shakes his head. 'They should let you children go too. I shall ask them, when I can.'

'Thank you,' David says. '*Shukran.*'

The little boy, unsettled by his mother's crying, starts trying to climb out of his seat, so the man turns away to deal with him.

I really don't want them to go. 'David,' I say, 'I don't . . .' A sob escapes.

He puts an arm round me. 'Neither do I. Maybe they can help once they're off – you heard what he said.'

It all feels so unfair – so hopeless.

But it turns out that everything is not so simple for those leaving. The young couple behind are engaged. He's Arab and she's British. He can go, but she's told she has to stay. He gets up to talk to the captain. Sweaty comes and speaks to the two of them, while the woman sits ashen-faced. The two men speak in Arabic, and it's obvious that the man is refusing to go without his fiancée. Sweaty speaks directly to the woman, and she breaks down, begs him to let her go too. He refuses, raises his voice.

I can't stand it when he's nearby. The thought of him touching me again . . .

The man refuses to leave her, still insists she goes too. 'We're getting married in a few days. In England!' he says again and again.

Sweaty shakes his head. He's standing right beside David now. I can see his expression. *He's enjoying it, the power he has*

70

over them. The bastard. The woman starts to sob. The man sits down to comfort her. The Giant arrives, listens and then relents, says she can leave with him. The man stands up, shakes the Giant's hand, looks overjoyed, then returns to his fiancée.

Before Sweaty and the Giant go, the Arab man opposite stands up, and with great dignity addresses them formally in Arabic. He keeps gesturing towards us, and for a moment I feel a surge of hope. Can we leave too? Will this all be over soon? But the Giant and Sweaty are adamant. We stay. Sweaty points to his watch and walks away. The Arab man sits down, defeated. His wife, who has already packed up their things, leans over and pats his arm. I want to thank him for trying, but feel so incredibly disappointed.

All hope of escape has gone.

The couple behind follow the hijackers to the front to speak to the captain about arrangements for leaving, and Tim slips into his seat beside me.

'Blimey, what was all that racket about?'

David ignores him. 'It's really not fair,' he says. 'Just because she's in love with an Arab, she's allowed to go. Maybe I'm half Arab but have a British passport.'

'Are you half Arab?' Tim looks fascinated.

'No, I'm not. But that's not the point. They're bending the rules, just for her. Who's making up these rules anyway? What about saying anyone under eighteen can go too.'

'Well, I think it's good that they're bending them,' I say. 'If they're letting her go, maybe they'll bend them for us at some point.'

'Fat chance,' David says grumpily. Then, 'I know, I know, I'm jealous. But it just doesn't feel fair. What have we done wrong? Why's her life more important than mine or yours or Tim's?'

'Well, at least some people are getting off,' Tim says.

'Exactly,' I say. 'If some can, then maybe...' I trail off.

'We can?' Tim says brightly.

'Yes, maybe we can.'

The Arab family stand in the aisle. The man smiles, leans over and shakes each of us by the hand. The woman waves from behind him. The little boy, still clutching his VW Beetle, sits on her hip, his arm looped round his mother's. He looks solemnly at us with big brown eyes. I try to smile, to make him smile back, but my heart isn't in it. There was something comforting about having that family across the aisle.

'I liked them,' Tim says wistfully after they've gone.

'Me too,' I say and we all fall silent.

I decide to slide across the aisle into the three empty seats. The family is down under the plane waiting for the minibus to take them away. The engaged couple stand hand in hand behind them. Through the window I see them climb into a battered old bus and drive away in a cloud of dust. Then I lie down across their three seats and try to doze.

13

18.20 hrs

It's late afternoon and still unbearably hot; the air is thick and heavy and I'm dying for a drink. Since the others left the plane, a feeling of stagnation has set in. Nothing seems to be happening. No one bothers to move about much. It's as if we've been sucked into the black hole of despondency.

I'm in the footwell under the three empty seats, sticky with sweat, lying stretched out on my back with one arm over my eyes, trying and failing to sleep. Tim's curled up in his seat by the window opposite and David's snoozing with his feet on my old seat.

I had thought it would be great to lie here across the three empty seats, but the last metal armrest by the window is fixed, so my feet hung in the aisle for people to knock as they went by. And if I lay on my side, the seatbelts dug into my shoulders and back. So I'm squeezed down here on the floor, with the metal grille that runs down the length of the plane right by my head; my hair caught in it earlier when I turned over, making me wince in pain.

I try to imagine the cool late-afternoon sea breeze up on the roof of our house in Bahrain, the boys arguing over some cricket catch, or drinking jungle juice at the kitchen table or stealing ice cream from the freezer compartment of the fridge.

How long will it take before I forget what they look like?

I sit up, scramble into the window seat and stare out to where the hard sand meets the scrubland. Sam took off once into the desert from the house. Left home. He was only four. We'd been teasing him, loading his lunch plate up with leftovers, calling him *the dustbin*, saying he had to eat all of it. Suddenly he got up and left the room. We looked at each other, stunned.

'He'll be all right,' Marni said. 'Just give him time to cool down.' But he reappeared with a small bag over one shoulder, his beloved tiger bulging inside it. He went into the kitchen, took a small coloured bottle and stood on a chair to fill it with water. No one said a word as he opened the front door and left. We just crowded round the window. And there he was, marching steadily out across the wasteland, a small figure wearing shorts and flip-flops. I remember how we expected him to stop, to lose his nerve. But he didn't. He just kept going.

'Quick!' Marni said to Mark. 'Run after him. Tell him we're sorry. *Really* sorry. Tell him we'd like him to come back so that we can apologise properly. Did you get that?'

'Yes,' shouted Mark, scampering off.

'I think we'd better be a bit more sensitive,' Marni said. 'When he returns, no smiling when you apologise. Especially you, James!'

'I promise,' Dad said with a smile.

And I'm overcome by a great wave of grief, of missing them. Missing everything: the lines that fan round Dad's eyes when he smiles, the way Marni's eyes light up and laugh on their own.

I remember standing on the top diving board overlooking the tennis courts last week. Dad had his toe on the baseline and both arms up in the air, one holding the tilted racket, his eyes gazing upwards at the soft white ball, frozen for a split second before the explosion of his serve. And Mark was below in the pool splashing Sam, and Marni was sitting on the side, sipping orange from a frosted bottle with a white paper straw. And I was with them.

Now I'm left just trying to imagine them.

14

18.25 hrs

I'm startled by the captain's voice. He's saying that the guards have insisted we have a rota to get fresh air at the open door, that we can only go in ones and twos and only stay for a few minutes each.

David asks if I'm up to going again, offers to put my name down for me if I like. I say I'll go with him, but not alone.

When it's our turn, we sit on the black seat by the open door and look out. A slant of hot sun burns my knees. David's amazed to see the other plane.

'If I sit and dangle my feet out,' he says, 'I might be able to see the third one.'

'I wouldn't,' I say quickly. 'Don't make them angry again.'

I look at the low hills breaking the skyline, run my eye along the length of them, as far as I can see and back again, trying to memorise the rise and fall, the edge and shift of them, like I'm drawing them with a soft pencil or charcoal. Along . . . and then back.

There's something soothing in it.

'God, I'm thirsty.' David is staring disconsolately out into the desert. 'And I heard that guy Alan say that they've run out of soft drinks and there's no water at all now.'

'They can't leave us here with nothing to drink.' I look at him. 'Can they?'

'They seem to be. Can you see over there?' He points. 'Don't you think they look like trenches, like they've dug them round the plane?'

'Yes, but are you sure they're trenches? D'you think the guerrillas live in them? Like in the First World War? Trenches like that?'

'Sort of,' David says, 'though smaller, more temporary. I suppose if they were billeted above ground they might get picked off by snipers or something. Have you noticed the hills on the other side of the plane? God knows who or what might come up from behind them.'

'What do you mean?' I hadn't even thought about it. He's making me feel really uneasy. 'Everyone says that the Palestinians have control of this area.'

'Yes, for now,' he says. 'But what if the Americans decide to attack, or the British, or the King of Jordan's army? He must be keen to get control of his country back.'

'For God's sake,' I say. I stare out into the desert. 'We're not in a very good position, are we?'

'Not great,' he says.

'Do you think the captain and the people in first class know more about what's happening than they're telling us?'

'God knows.' David sighs. 'It's going to be weird, if we do get out, going back after this, isn't it?' he says.

'Mmm.'

'Got my mocks coming up.'

'What in?'

'Physics, chemistry and biology.'

'A scientist then.'

'Yeah. I want to do medicine. Dad's a doctor and all three of his brothers too. So there's no escape.'

'I see what you mean.'

'What about your . . . Hey!' he says suddenly. 'Look! Can you see them? There. Those dots.' Way out on the far horizon a number of tiny black shapes are moving about. We watch, fascinated. Slowly, very slowly, they take shape and materialise into a semicircle of tanks.

'My God! I can see the guns,' I say.

'They can't be the PFLP's,' David says. 'I doubt if they have any.'

'Alan said they'd heard on the news that the King of Jordan is coming with tanks. Or what about the Syrians?' I suggest. 'He said they were massing tanks on the Jordanian border.'

'Are you serious?' David looks shocked. 'Then let's hope they *are* the King of Jordan's, otherwise we're going to be not just in the middle of a civil war, but a full-scale international one.'

My heart skips a beat. A civil war, families fighting families, or a full-scale war? And us in the middle.

'Look,' David says. 'Can you see? All the tanks have their guns trained on us.'

We watch the sun sink, turning the sky a washed-out blue and the sand a gentle peach, like the colour of the face powder in Marni's compact. Soon a fiery sun sets, glowing behind the line of hills, etching them onto the back of my eye, so that when I blink they're still there.

15

19.00 hrs

As the temperature in the cabin drops, the warm, wet sweat that we've grown so used to cools. My shirt becomes clammy and it's a relief to begin with, but then I feel cold. The guerrillas all wear thick jumpers, but few of us have anything. Some people have winter coats, which they pull down off the luggage racks and put on. I'm beginning to wish I had some of my school uniform, but it's in my case in the luggage hold.

We've still been given nothing to drink. There's plenty of alcohol, but no soft drinks or water left. My throat's parched, and there's a small hammer tapping at the back of my head. I hope they hurry and find water for us tonight. I can actually feel myself shrivelling up, dehydrating. Now I understand what being 'dry as a bone' means.

It's dark in the cabin. Several hurricane lamps have been passed up from outside. The Giant and Sweaty are lighting them at the front and hanging them at intervals down the plane by hooking them over the edges of the ceiling recesses. They fill the cabin with their hissing and dance about when people walk to and fro, casting strange elongated shadows.

The Giant and the captain are hanging one right above our seats.

'Are you sure these are safe with all the explosives about?' the captain asks. 'What if one falls and catches fire?'

The Giant smiles in his own quiet way and assures him that they'll be all right.

I'm not so sure. But it looks as if we have more than that to worry about right now. The Giant looks down at the captain, then hesitates and frowns. 'I have just been told that the second-in-command is coming on board. To speak to everyone.'

The captain gives him a quizzical look. 'Second-in-command?'

'Yes, she is coming,' he repeats, as if that explains everything. 'Everyone must be seated.'

The captain goes to the front and asks everyone to return to their seats. David glances over, catches my eye and makes a *what now?* face. I shrug, twist round in my chair and look back down the plane. The two guards are hurrying the last few people to their seats. Mrs Green looks anxiously at Susan, who whispers secrets into her rag doll's ear. Mrs Newton, swaying slightly, is still fussing in her overhead locker. When I turn to the front again, the Giant and Sweaty have completely disappeared. The captain, looking drawn, waits patiently until everyone is seated, then he too sits down.

A figure climbs aboard: a woman wearing khaki fatigues, black boots and a red-and-white checked scarf wound loosely around her head. She's very striking, with strong features, dark eyes and arched brows. She stands at the front, her face lit by the overhead lanterns, nods curtly at the captain, then stares out at us, shifting her gaze from face to face, taking her time. The conversation in the cabin peters out and the atmosphere changes, as if something new and more hostile has entered the plane. And now I don't want to be sitting here on my own. I want to be back between Tim and David.

Two new guards follow the woman in and stand on either side of her. One is heavy-shouldered with a bullneck and rough complexion; the other is tall with wary deep-set eyes and an oversized jaw. Both wear immaculate fatigues and have sub-machine guns slung across their shoulders.

She starts speaking, slowly and deliberately, in perfect English with a faint Arab accent. 'We have brought you here because we planned it. We have guns, bombs, hand grenades. We are strong.' She pauses, to let her words sink in. 'You, on the other hand, are helpless. Trapped.'

The cabin is deathly quiet except for the hissing lamps. I glance at David, who widens his eyes at me.

She starts pacing a little, pushing her head forward, emphasising each word. 'We will live. We have water and food. You will be hungry, thirsty. We will live, and – if we choose – you will die.'

I feel a bolt of shock. Why is she doing this? None of the other hijackers have spoken like this. Not the Giant, not even Sweaty. Her two guards stand cold and impassive, their belts heavy with grenades. Are they going to kill us now? Mow us down? Is that what she is saying? Why would she speak like this otherwise? My mind whirls. I feel disbelief and panic. I feel sick.

'Excuse me.' The captain stands up.

The woman swings round. 'What?' she spits.

'We have children on board.'

'You?' she says. '*You* tell *me* about children?' In one fluid movement, she pulls the pistol from her belt, cocks it and points it at his head. 'You tell me about children?' she shouts. 'What about us? What about our children? What about them? The ones who died at the hands of the murdering invaders? Do they not count?'

'Of course they count,' the captain says quietly, his face white.

'Silence!' she screams. 'You are nothing here! Silence! Or you will be removed! SIT!'

He sits.

A horrid quiet seeps back.

She lowers her gun and begins to speak again, her voice thick with hatred. 'The murderers took our land and threw us onto the scrapheap of the world.' I feel her seething disgust as she paces down the aisle towards the back of the plane. 'And who cares? No one!' She turns and comes forward again. 'So we have risen up. AND WE WILL BE HEARD!' she yells.

The hurricane lamps jiggle crazily as she stalks past. 'If your Prime Minister doesn't release our comrade Leila Khaled in London by midday on Saturday, you will ALL DIE. We will blow up the whole plane with you in it.' She spins around at the front. 'Or maybe,' she adds, lowering her voice and leaning forward, 'we will kill you all, one...by...one.'

Oh God. Oh God.

She raises her head, gives us a triumphant look, turns on her heel and leaves the plane, followed by her two guards.

There's a stunned silence, as if all the air on the plane has been sucked out.

I look at David, staring at the seat in front, at Tim, clutching Fred's tin on his lap. I watch them in a dream, unable to move.

There's murmuring. It grows from muttering into outrage then sheer panic. Mr and Mrs Newton stagger to the front, walking painfully, looking as if they have aged. More adults move forward in drifts.

The two guards at the back do nothing as the crowd at the front increases. Passengers lean over seat backs, stand in the aisle, sit on the seat arms, crowding in and around the captain and the crew in first class. The captain stands up and starts to speak, softly at first, then with more strength. He's trying to reassure us, desperately trying to quieten the growing hysteria in the cabin.

'Who does she think she is?' roars Mr Newton. 'Coming in here and threatening us like that? Lady Bloody Macbeth?'

16

Thursday 10th September 1970

Revolutionary Airstrip, Jordan - 05.00 hrs

It's the second day. The first light streaming into the plane wakes me. I lie still, disturbed by my dream. I'd been shut in a cardboard box with only small holes to let the light in. I knew I had to get out quickly, but I couldn't move my arms or legs.

I sit up slowly. My whole body feels bruised and battered. My eyes are like lead, my neck stiff, my head aches.

No one else seems to be awake. David's asleep, sitting upright but skewed over, with his feet in the aisle and his mouth open. Tim's curled up next to him, like a dormouse. I can see the edge of Fred's tin under his seat. It's funny, I feel like I've known them for ages, but it's only been one day.

I started the night crunched up on my empty seats, struggling to avoid the armrests and belts digging into my back. Rosemary warned us about the sudden temperature drop at night, and I was desperately cold in my thin cotton miniskirt and T-shirt, despite the BOAC blankets she gave out.

Every time I turned over, I exposed a foot, an arm or a shoulder, and woke freezing, aching with it. The end of my nose, my hands and my feet were numb. At one stage I couldn't feel my arm at all and woke up shivering, my teeth chattering like I'd been locked in a freezer. I literally couldn't sit still. Had to walk up and down to get warm. I couldn't stop thinking about my school coat. I longed for the intense heat of yesterday.

Thinking it might be warmer down there, I crawled into the footwell under the seats, but the freezing metal feet tormented me at every turn. I've never slept in the desert before. The temperature drop must be crazy. In Bahrain we needed fans at night it was so hot, and only slept under one thin sheet.

There's heavy snoring coming from way back, probably the Newtons after all that whisky. I can't see any guards. Maybe they're sitting in the doorway. In the pauses between snores I can hear the plane ticking, like it's expanding in the sun after the cold night. I imagine it like a great restless bird wanting to be back up there in the blue sky instead of being manacled down here on earth.

I look at my watch. Five o'clock. What will happen now after that awful woman's visit last night? I reach over and pull the window cover up. The sky's washed a delicate pink. The sun, edged in fire, burns low on the horizon. Some of the guerrillas are milling about down below, squatting on the ground, smoking, chatting; doing what people on a campsite do at first light. One stands and stretches, pulls on his jacket and tucks a rolled towel under his arm. There are two men by a parked Jeep, changing a tyre, the contents of their toolbox spewed out on the sand.

My stomach suddenly cramps. I double over until the pain passes, and am left feeling more sick and empty than ever before. My head is really killing me now. Must be dehydration. My lips are cracking, my tan is flaking off and my eyes feel shrunk-dry. My throat's parched. I am *so* thirsty. I hope they give us some water soon. I run a thick tongue around my furred teeth and gums. Disgusting. My tongue sticks to the roof of my mouth, like I've run out of saliva. Is that possible? How long can a human last without water? I'm sure it's only a matter of days.

Two guerrillas pass below laughing, their arms around each other's shoulders. What did my friends at school think when I didn't turn up yesterday? They'll have stayed up chatting all night. I feel a pang at missing them and hearing all their news.

I think about my best friend, Ali, with her crazy crooked smile. Seeing her is the best thing about going back. She's the funniest and the most loyal friend ever. She always brings me sheets of paper-thin dried apricot, looking like amber glass, back from Istanbul, where she lives. And there's Jaffa, obsessed with smoking and horses, with legs like a foal herself. I always smuggle in duty-free fags for her in my suitcase. And Fi, whose spoilt mother told her only to marry for money, and Spud, with her wild red hair, who hid in bed for days when her dad died last term. They'll all feel knackered, being woken by the bell at seven this morning. There'll be baths, prayers and breakfast in the old dining room, smelling of gravy, fried eggs and the porridge that sets like cement in your stomach. What I'd do for a bowl of that now, or even a cup of Matron's horrible metallic tea.

They'll do the long walk from the boarding house to Main School. It'll be cool, raining. They'll wear brown regulation macs, and troop along the wet pavements, talking and laughing. The mist will dampen their faces. The trees down the avenue will drip on their heads. The dew on the games pitches will soak their socks, but they'll just carry on, as normal, like all the people flocking to work and school on their buses and trains, cars and bikes.

A tiny iridescent fly lands on the top of the seat in front and proceeds to wash its antennae and smooth down its wings. Then, just as suddenly, it takes off again, flying down though the cabin – and probably out through the open door. Just like that. Easy. Because it can.

I think what it would be like to climb down the ladder and slip away, unnoticed, to Amman. Someone said there were roadblocks all the way into the capital, so I couldn't go that way. And crossing the desert would kill me. I'd wander round and round, lost and dried out and hopeless until I fell to the ground, like in the films, ending up like one of those carcasses you see in the desert, a sun-bleached ribcage with sand grains gusting through it.

Has anyone at home realised I'm missing? Have they been told what's happened? Marni must surely know by now. Marni... No, I can't think about her. Too hard. Too weakening. But maybe they watched the news last night. Maybe the Prime Minister made a statement outside Downing Street saying he would let the Palestinian woman go. Maybe we'll hear it on Mr Newton's radio later... Maybe...

Maybe...

God, I *have* to get back to sleep.

17

Bahrain - 07.00 hrs

Marni surfaces from a short fitful sleep. The last day, she thinks, turning over. Then her body jolts. It's a dream!

It's not a dream. Her eyes shoot open.

Anna.

Waves of panic wash over her. She throws back the covers, sits on the edge of the bed.

James? He said he'd go into the office to find out if there's any more news. They'd sat up most of the night worrying, waiting, hoping for the phone to ring with good news, news of Anna's release. But there was none.

The boys. I'll have to tell them now, can't keep it from them any longer.

She stands up, but grief empties her, sucks away all her energy. She slumps back down. What have they done to her? She sees Anna at gunpoint and shudders, heaves with the horror of it. A sob shakes her frame.

But the boys, I have to tell them.

They mustn't see me like this. I must be strong. She brushes away her tears. I must tell them before someone else does. Somehow. They mustn't be fearful about flying today.

Today. She gets up, pads past the luggage and the packing cases in the hall, past the boys' clothes laid out on the two dining-room chairs, and stands in the doorway of their room.

She pauses. Then she reaches up and switches off the overhead fan. Its turbulent rhythm immediately quietens. The whirring slows. It calms, slices through the air more and more slowly. She watches until the three blades are quite still.

She will never wake her boys here again. Nothing will be the same again.

The boys stir in the quiet. Mark turns and rubs his eyes.

'Mum?' She goes and kisses him, smooths his hair.

'Hello, my darling,' she says, stroking the small brown arm lying outside the covers and feeling comforted by its warmth, the life in it.

She goes and pulls the curtains open and kisses the small bundle of Sam.

'Good morning, my treasure,' she says, and sits on the edge of his bed. She touches his head, leans over to kiss him and hears the goat with the bell going by outside the fence.

Mark sits up, and when Sam sees him he struggles upright too. 'I'm hungry,' he says.

'Breakfast in a minute,' Marni replies. 'But, darlings, I've got something to tell you. It's not an easy thing.' She pauses. 'We had a phone call from Dad's boss. He says that some men have taken over Anna's plane, not the pilot or the crew, but some other men, hijackers.'

Mark concentrates on her, listening intently.

'Remember how we said hijackers were people who get on board someone else's plane and tell the captain to fly it to where they want to go?'

'Not to England?' says Sam.

'No.'

'Where have they taken it?' asks Mark.

'Well, they've told the captain of Anna's plane to fly to Jordan, near Jerusalem in the Holy Land.'

'Isn't that where Jesus lived?' says Sam.

'That's right,' Marni says.

'Mum,' says Mark, 'have they landed there?'

'Yes, darling, apparently they've landed in the desert somewhere not far from the capital, Amman. But that's all we know at the moment. Dad's gone to find out more before we fly.'

'We?' says Mark. 'Are you coming too?'

'Yes, we've been ordered to fly home today, to wait for Anna in England. Dad's boss said we should all go together, on an RAF flight.'

'Will we be hijacked?'

'No, Mark,' says Marni. 'Everyone will be extra careful to keep us safe, now that this has happened to Anna.'

'How long is she going to be there then?'

'Well, they're saying that they'll let Anna come home safely if the Prime Minister of England lets another hijacker go. One who is in prison in England.'

'If I was the captain,' Sam butts in, 'I'd fly the plane wherever I wanted to go. I wouldn't do what those people say.'

'I think the captain might have tried that.'

Mark looks at Marni. 'They've got guns, haven't they?

'I'm afraid so.'

Sam looks shocked. 'Are they going to shoot Anna?'

'No.' Marni's voice catches. 'But we don't have to think about that now, do we?'

'Can Dad go and get Anna back? With some of our soldiers who have guns too,' asks Sam.

'No, darling. He would if he thought they could. If it would work.'

'Why wouldn't it work?'

'Well, it's better that we leave it to the special people who know how to talk to hijackers. We don't want to upset them.' Marni feels it unwinding. She's getting into dangerous waters. She'll have to bring it to a close, let it all sink in. There'll be another raft of questions later. And she needs time to think how on earth she'll deal with them.

'Is Anna going to stay there a long time?' Mark asks.

'But she's all on her own!' Sam wails. 'She'll be sad!' He bursts into tears. Marni puts her arms round him. Mark climbs out of bed and comes to sit with them. He begins to cry quietly too. She feels their distress, a sharp pain in her heart.

'She's not going to die, is she?'

'No,' says Marni. She wavers, then feels angry. 'No. She's not. We won't let her, will we?' She says it a little too loud.

Mark stands up. 'I don't want to talk about it any more,' he says. 'I'm going onto the roof.' He picks up his violin case and leaves. And while Marni and Sam make breakfast together, the strains of a violin float down the stone stairwell.

18

Revolutionary Airstrip, Jordan - 09.00 hrs

When I wake again, I'm slumped sideways in my seat with the pattern of the material printed on my cheek. My neck and shoulders have seized up. When I move, I feel like I might crack in half. It's warmer now, thank God, and everyone seems to be awake.

What must I look like? I try running my fingers through my hair, but it's far worse now, really thick with tangles. How stupid to forget to bring a brush. It's always so matted in the mornings. When I was little Marni would spend ages trying to brush the knots out, and to distract me from the tugging would say that the fairies had been dancing in it again in the night. And I'd feel proud to have been chosen by them.

'Nice hairdo.' David's grinning face appears over the top of the seat behind.

'Thanks.'

'I thought beehives had gone out.'

'Er...' I nod at his hair.

'It's the new look,' he says. '*Wild hostage*. Tim hasn't quite got the hang of it yet, have you, Tim?' Tim pops his head up. 'He's still sporting the *Prep School*: a practical cut that stays put in extreme situations.' Tim's expression is so impish, he'd look perfect sitting on a toadstool.

David nods at my window. 'You seen out there yet?'

'No...' I shift over and look. 'Blimey!'

Fifty yards from the plane are hundreds of reporters sitting on the sand surrounded by all their stuff: camera bags, lenses, tape recorders, microphones, folding ladders, TV booms...

'Yes, the world's press has arrived!' David says ceremoniously.

'What d'you think they'll do?' I ask.

'Take pictures?' he suggests.

Tim's eyes light up. 'So we'll be allowed off?'

'I doubt it,' David says. 'After all, we might make a run for it.'

There's a brief moment while we all consider the possibility, then discard it.

'How did you sleep?' David asks.

'Dreadfully.' I yawn. 'Tried under the seats too.'

'I might try that tonight,' he says. 'Is there room for two down there?'

I roll my eyes. 'There's hardly room for one.'

'Hey! Look,' Tim says. 'Something's happening.'

We crowd around the windows. A tall man, wearing traditional dress, a long crisp white cotton *thawb* and a black-and-white keffiyeh headscarf, walks out from under the plane holding a loudspeaker. He stops directly in front of the crowd of reporters and raises his hand, waiting for silence. Then he starts addressing the reporters who either listen intently, film him, or take notes.

'Wish we could hear what he's saying,' David says, exasperated.

'I know, it's really annoying. It sounds blurry, like we're in a fishbowl.'

'God,' he says, 'we're always the last to know everything.'

After a few minutes, the man leaves and the reporters stand and brush themselves down. They start collecting up their things, shifting into groups. Some stay talking to each other, others file towards our plane and form a queue by the ladder.

At the front, the captain gets to his feet and addresses us. 'Good morning, everyone,' he says. 'I hope your night wasn't too uncomfortable. As you can see, we've got visitors. I've been asked to tell you all to stay seated while they come aboard to interview some of us and take film footage for TV. Please be as helpful as you can. We need the rest of the world to know what's happening here. This may very well help to secure our freedom.'

Behind him, the Giant puts down his gun and goes to help the first reporter up into the plane. He's a large, plump man with a shock of white hair, wearing a crumpled khaki safari suit. A TV camera is passed up after him. Every pocket of his suit, and there are many, bulges with pieces of equipment. He takes the camera and stands next to Sweaty in the aisle. When he turns round to look for his colleague, we see two patches of red sand on his buttocks where he's been sitting in the desert.

'Hi,' he calls out to us, still panting slightly after climbing the ladder. 'We've come to take pictures of you, to interview you for the papers and the TV. But the guerrillas have only given us a short time slot each, so please stay sitting down while we file by you. There's a helluva lot of us to get on, through this plane and out the back door.'

He makes it sound like a jolly outing. Does he realise how lucky he is to come and go so freely?

Sweaty and the Giant wave up more reporters. They come in groups of two or three and move down the aisle, to be escorted off by the two guards at the back door, where I suppose they've got another ladder. Some of them speak to the captain, others move on down the plane towards us, choosing someone to question, maybe to record and film. The aisle fills up. There's no room anywhere. It's getting hotter and hotter. There's no air left.

But I need to be filmed. Then the others will see I'm alive, that I'm all right.

Ask me, I plead silently. But they just walk past.

Eventually, a tall, blond man with a pointed beard and a thin, leathery woman in a bright white shirt start to film me. They're from a Swedish TV station.

'Pretend to sleep, please,' the woman instructs me.

I close my eyes and listen to the camera whirr. But instead of feeling good, I feel awkward, confused, embarrassed even. *What am I doing?* Pretending to sleep, while strangers stare at me, filming?

Why haven't they asked if I'm OK? Asked my name? Why haven't they offered to help, to take a message back? Don't they think I might need to contact my family?

I should say something. But what?

I'm beginning to feel really stupid. What will my family, or my friends at school think, if they see the clip of me asleep on TV? That I'm relaxed and enjoying myself?

Or dead?

I'm on show. An animal in the zoo. A specimen.

My mind starts to unravel. Anger courses through me. I open my eyes.

'No, no! Close your eyes,' the man cries.

'I'm not . . .' But I crumple, feel tearful, weak, '. . . sleepy.'

The man and the woman stare at me for a moment, then shrug and move down the plane to film someone else.

19

10.30 hrs

After all the reporters have finished going through the plane, Rosemary appears with a tray. A water ration! I take one of the tiny paper cups and look at the rippling, silver surface, wondering, just for a split second, whether I should dip my fingers in and wash my face?

No, I must drink it all. I need it. I sip tiny, tiny sips very, very slowly, but too soon the cup is empty...

The captain has been picking small groups to go down and be filmed in the desert by the reporters. I watched enviously as the two blonde girls left and came back laughing, and the bald man and the redhead in first class have just returned too. The captain comes down the cabin and stops by the three of us. 'Fancy a walk in the desert?' he says.

'Yes, please!' cries Tim.

David jumps up. 'Fantastic! Anything to get out of here for a bit!'

But suddenly, just for a split second, I hesitate. The idea of leaving the plane feels dangerous. They're all looking at me.

David looks perplexed. 'Come on, Anna!'

I get up.

Heads turn to watch as we follow the captain up the aisle. I waft through the bald man's cloud of cigar smoke in first class, and, as I wait for the captain and Jim, and then David and Tim, to climb down, I look back along the plane. Rosemary smiles and waves encouragingly, the two blonde sisters are arguing now and, further back, the twins' heads bob up and down, up and down, like they're part of a manic puppet show.

I stand in the doorway, watching the others move a little way off from the guards waiting at the bottom. Now it's my turn to go down. I wish I was wearing shorts, not my miniskirt. Hoping desperately that no one is looking up, I start climbing down the rough wooden ladder propped against the plane. I try to hold my skirt down as well as the rope slanting alongside, but the rope wobbles so violently I have to let go and hold on to the ladder with both hands. God, this is so embarrassing. Which is worse – Sweaty seeing my knickers or David? It's a long way down. The sun's heat burns the back of my legs.

Strong arms help me down the last bit. I feel the metal bed of the Jeep under my feet and turn round. The young guy whose ammo belt I got caught on looks solemnly down at me, his eyes a startling green. I blush and thank him. *Shukran.* He immediately springs down onto the sand and holds out both hands to help me down again.

I withdraw my hands as quickly as I can, covered with confusion. He smiles and his face lights up, quite transformed.

I'm relieved to feel the hard, compacted sand under my feet, but the light here is blinding, and the desert wind hot and relentless. I screw up my eyes and peer far off, at the wavering heat sheen distorting the horizon.

I turn and squint up at the great smooth white body of the plane shining high overhead, see the thick stripe down the side and the great, tapered, swept-back wings reaching out well down the body. I look up at the navy nose cone with its slanting rectangular windows, at the windscreen wipers lying still and quiet on the glass, and feel the enormous majestic plane looking softly down at me.

A huge Palestinian flag has been draped alongside the open door. Its red triangle with black, white and green stripes ripples in the hot wind. Above it, painted in black, are the letters *P.F.L.P.* – the Popular Front for the Liberation of Palestine.

The sun beats down on my head. Instinctively I step back into the shade under the plane where the others are sheltering.

'Och yes, she's a great flyer,' Jim's telling David and Tim, 'especially in hot and humid countries. She's perfectly made for high-speed landings and takeoffs.' He looks up at the plane's underbelly. 'Her body shrinks and expands in the heat and cold, you know.'

'What? A lot?' Tim asks.

'Aye – well, enough.' Jim grins. 'Looks like it's our turn.' The captain is about to be led away to talk to the reporters. Jim catches up with him. Two guerrillas take them over to the crowd of reporters ranged behind a makeshift cordon of rope. Cameras click continuously as they approach. Some reporters have their notepads out; others are filming. Someone calls out a question.

'Yes,' the captain says, somehow managing to look dignified in his crumpled shirt. 'We were ordered to shut the engines down, which means no water, toilets or air conditioning. The passengers are very uncomfortable. The heat during the day, as you can imagine, is pretty awful, and at night it's extremely cold. During the day we open the escape hatches when we can, to let more air in. We've had no proper food since we landed, despite the Red Cross meals that are apparently waiting for us in Beirut. And, although we have a little water at the moment, it's having to be severely rationed.'

'Do you know what's going on back in London?' a man holding a clipboard shouts.

'We know we face the possibility of being blown up if the British government doesn't release Leila Khaled by midday on Saturday.'

It's Jim's turn to answer questions. He steps forward, the back of his shirt dark with sweat.

'Can you tell us what it was like landing the VC10 in the middle of the desert?' a man in mirror sunglasses calls.

'Well, it wasn't quite what we were expecting to be doing, but luckily the ground was firm, thank God. The main risk was running out of fuel before we located the landing strip.'

'How are you all coping with the deadline?' a woman calls.

'Not too badly. We have a day or so yet.'

'So how are you coping otherwise?' she insists.

'Ah, well, things turned a bit nasty last night, but soon calmed down. We're finding the lack of food and drink difficult, but generally we're managing to keep our spirits up.'

'Can we have a shot of those three kids under the plane now?' a man holding a TV camera shouts.

'A *shot*,' mutters David. 'Subtle.'

'One of them filming earlier,' Tim says, 'asked if I was missing my parents.'

'What did you say?'

'I said of course I wasn't.'

'What? Why? Was that wise?' I ask.

'It's our code,' Tim replies. 'Dad'll know. We always say we're not missing each other when we are.'

How I wish that I could send a message to Marni, coded or not. I look at the press jostling for position behind their rope, and wish I had the guts to shout something out to them. Maybe, if I could get closer, I could ask them to contact my family. But where? In Bahrain? In the UK? Where?

At least I'll have my picture taken. In the end, that may be the best message I can send: a picture of me alive – if they ever see it. We wait for Jim and the captain to be escorted back to us.

I look at the reporters, so busy with their equipment. 'They aren't *really* interested in what this feels like, are they?' I say to David.

'No,' he agrees. 'They're just out here to get their story, and the story is . . . we're going to be blown up.'

'David!' I give him a *not in front of the children* look. He opens his mouth to reply, but Sweaty pushes us from behind, out into the searingly bright sunlight.

Now I can see the luggage piled up under the wing and the circular grilles on the engines whirling in the wind. And further off, the TWA plane parked behind us.

The photographers are shouting instructions and pointing. 'Further to the right, no, further, yes, more, no, there.' We obey wordlessly, squinting into the sun at the banks of cameras.

We must look like we're just out for a stroll in the desert.

I glance back at the captain and Jim sheltering under the plane, see the two other planes shimmering in the distance and our three distorted shadows slanting a long, long way behind us. We stop, as directed, with our plane behind us, its wings outstretched like a huge mother bird.

As we stand there in the desert, I feel the hot wind sucking the moisture from the land, and from my body. It ripples my T-shirt, tugs at my skirt, flipping the wrap-over open. I try holding it down with one hand, but the wind tosses my hair up around my head, into my eyes. I reach with the other hand and hold my hair down behind my neck in a ponytail. Gritty sand whisked up by the wind stings my legs and arms. I screw up my eyes against the sun. And the cameras continue to whirr and click, click and whirr.

All too soon I'm back on the plane, wondering what happened out there. What it was all about. And what good it will do us.

I lie across my three seats, feeling exhausted and wondering when and if I'll ever leave the plane again. My head throbs now, my arms and legs ache. I'm so hungry, so empty that I feel as if I have no substance, that I've been completely hollowed out.

And I think how crazy it is that the reporters managed to get here, to Amman, and out into the desert to come aboard the plane, but no one thought about bringing us the meals from Beirut, or any water – or anything.

I watch the reporters packing up their photographic gear and climbing back into their minibuses and I feel disappointed, betrayed even. If this was a movie, we'd have been rescued by now. But it's not a movie, it's real, and no one can possibly rescue us with all these explosives on board.

A man walks up and down, slamming the minibus doors shut. Then they're off, snaking their way across the desert, until the last one disappears in a trail of red dust. The dust settles and the desert is still again. And it's as if none of them were ever here.

20

12.00 hrs

Rosemary sits down in the empty aisle seat and drops several long packets of duty-free cigarettes into the seat between us. 'Phew! It's hot!' she says. 'We're nearly out of duty-free now. I can't offer a meal, so may as well keep everyone's spirits up. And these are the last few packets of cigarettes. Everyone's smoking like chimneys, have you noticed? Do you want any? Do you smoke?'

'Only occasionally,' I say. 'And not in front of my parents.'

'Well, you're welcome to have one of these. A present for someone when you get home, perhaps.' She passes over a carton of 200 Rothmans.

'Thanks.'

'Tim was funny,' Rosemary says. 'He asked if he could take some to give to his dad.'

'Really? And did you give him some?'

'I'm afraid I did. I didn't want to ruin his reputation in front of the twins.'

'They look so sweet.'

'Yes, they are. Quite mischievous too.' Rosemary looks at me. 'How are you doing?'

'Oh, all right . . .' I hesitate.

'I heard about you and the skinny hijacker.' Rosemary grimaces.

I shrug, non-committal. She's so nice, but I wish she wouldn't be kind. It reminds me of Marni and makes everything much more difficult, pierces my hopelessly thin armour.

'Hungry, I expect.'

'Mmm, and thirsty,' I say.

'You know they're promising us food tonight.'

I look up. 'That's good. If we can wait that long!'

'Did I hear the word food?' David swings into the aisle seat opposite.

'Only *some*,' Rosemary says. 'And frankly, I'll believe it when I see it. I don't want to raise your hopes. Up at the front, we've been distracting each other with recipes.'

David groans. 'That sounds like torture.'

'My mother's sherry trifle and the curry in the officers' mess were definite favourites,' Rosemary says.

'Don't, *please*,' David says.

'Oh, and bacon sarnies,' she adds.

'Oh God. I can smell them.' David closes his eyes and swallows.

'Spaghetti Bolognese with grated Parmesan,' I say. 'Then home-made vanilla ice cream . . .'

'Ah . . . with melted chocolate on top!' adds Rosemary.

'*So* cruel!' David grimaces. But then he grins at us. 'I'd have – a hamburger and chips with loads of tomato sauce, or a great slab of steak, grilled mushrooms, garlic butter . . .' He stops and shakes his head. 'Now I *really* know what it feels like when your stomach caves in.'

I glance out of my window, at the circle of Jeeps and the tanks beyond. 'Are they definitely the King of Jordan's tanks, Rosemary?'

'Yes.'

'Why are the guns trained on us then?' I say. 'They can hardly pick off the hijackers, so what's going on?'

'I don't know. But we've been talking to the very tall hijacker.'

'The Giant,' I say.

She laughs. 'Yes. He says all his comrades are Palestinians who've been living in refugee camps here in Jordan for years and years, ever since they were forced out of Palestine. They think that the rest of the world has ignored what's happened to them, so this is what they've had to do to get attention – and help. They're desperate, he says, otherwise they wouldn't be doing it, and they are hoping against hope that someone will help them return to their homes in Palestine. They say they've been driven to take action, including taking over areas of Jordan and putting up roadblocks, so the King of Jordan's making his presence felt with those tanks. I just hope it doesn't end up in a civil war.'

'Are they actually fighting each other?' David asks.

'I don't think so, not yet, but we don't really know. Syria, on the other border, are looking like they might get involved.'

'Invade Jordan?' I say.

'Possibly.'

'Why?'

'I don't know. To stop the unrest?'

'Then we'll be in the middle of a war as well!'

'Well, let's hope not.' But she doesn't sound sure.

'So all we can do is sit here,' I say, feeling desperate, 'and wait for it to happen?'

'Well, not entirely.' Rosemary smiles. 'The captain's arranging for each of us to send a telegram to Ted Heath.'

'Ted Heath, the Prime Minister?'

'Yes, the British Prime Minister, to try to persuade him to release the Palestinian terrorist captured in London. The hijackers are obviously behind the idea too.'

'Was she the one on the Israeli plane flying from Amsterdam?' I ask.

'Yes, to New York. It was rerouted to London. D'you know, Leila Khaled is only twenty-something, my age – imagine. Apparently she wears a ring made from a bullet.'

What happens to make you end up hijacking a plane in your early twenties? I wonder. Something *very* serious. And what can it be like to be made to leave your home and country? Become homeless? I really want to know, to make sense of it. I know what it's like to move so often, but we always have a home to go to. We always have a choice.

'Celia! Where's Rosemary?' It's Mr Newton and he sounds very drunk. 'Yes, Rosemary.' His voice is querulous. 'I want her. She promised me . . .'

Rosemary stands up. 'I'd better go. I'm not sure that Celia should have given the Newtons an entire bottle of whisky. They've drunk half of it already.'

21

13.00 hrs

Tim's spending more and more time with the twins. They've all rolled up their sleeves and walk round with their school shirts unbuttoned and flapping to try to keep cool. Lucky them, I say. I even heard Tim begging Rosemary to cut the legs off his school trousers.

He says the twins are very impressed with Fred. They have an agreement: if they can have Fred sitting on their table with the lid open, they'll let Tim read their comics. He doesn't let Fred out of his sight though. Ever. They've also swapped their Spirograph for his Etch-A-Sketch, and right now the three of them are talking to each other up and down the aisle on walkie-talkies.

David has gone to play Monopoly with Alan and Rosemary in first class. I couldn't bear the thought of it. The talk of war has made me feel even more jittery and anxious. All I want to do is cut out and sleep. I don't want to think any more about anything – just for a while.

But it's *so* hot. The air hangs heavily in the cabin. The temperature's reached 140 °F outside already and everyone's sweating continuously. Some people's hair is plastered to their heads like they've just got out of the swimming pool. Sweat runs into our eyes all the time, and those in glasses have to wipe them continuously as they steam up in the heat. Eye make-up runs too, so most women have given up wearing any.

The cabin smells of hot plastic, smoky upholstery and stale sweat. Our clothes stink too, but what can we do? We're all in the same boat – well, plane. And the thirst is unbearable. My throat's so sore now that my voice has gone all croaky and it's a real effort to talk. *When* are they going to bring us another water ration? It's got to be soon.

And now, to add to all that, a revolting smell is wafting up the aisle from the toilets. There's been no water to flush them for hours. The last time I went, they were almost overflowing, but that was nothing compared to this. Looks like the captain and Jim are trying to sort something out with Sweaty and the Giant.

A child's walkie-talkie crackles quietly behind me. It's Tim, creeping backwards down the aisle. When he's alongside me, he stops.

'Pooh,' he says, 'the bogs *really* stink.'

'I know, it's disgusting. Let's hope they can sort it out soon.'

'Come in, number two,' Tim says into his walkie-talkie. 'Do you read me? Am in very stinky situation. Meet me at Row 5.'

When I do finally manage to snooze, David wakes me, desperate to tell me what's happened while I've been asleep. He's grinning from ear to ear.

'You've missed the funniest thing ever, Anna,' he says.

109

'What happened?'

'Well, the captain told the hijackers that the sewage pumps aren't working because the engine's switched off, and apparently the tanks weren't emptied in Beirut, so he said they have to empty them now somehow because those toilets are horrendous. He told them the waste chute's at the back of the plane and that they'd have to dig a pit below it and then unscrew the cap. But Sweaty said the captain and Jim should dig the pit. In this heat. They weren't happy about it.'

Tim comes by and stays to listen.

'So Jim and the captain climbed down the ladder and had to dig a pit with these small shovels while all the hijackers watched. It took them a while, and when the pit was big enough, Jim pointed to the sewage stopper and showed Sweaty how he couldn't reach it, and the captain did the same. So finally a tall, lanky guerrilla arrived with this other hijacker, who climbs up on his shoulders. Jim and the captain stand well away from the pit as the two men wobble towards the stopper. When they're underneath it, the man on top reaches up and starts turning the metal rim of the lid holding all the sewage inside the chute. And whoosh! Out spurts a great stream of it!'

Tim and David are laughing hysterically. 'Totally covered from head to toe in poo!'

'That is *so* disgusting!' Tim grins.

'Yes, they weren't best pleased.' David grins. 'Check out Sweaty's face. They're all so annoyed. When they got back on board, Jim and the captain couldn't stop laughing. They said they knew it would happen all along, and sure enough...! They were so funny. They sounded just like two naughty schoolkids.'

22

14.00 hrs

The captain has just repeated that unless Leila Khaled, the Palestinian hijacker imprisoned in London, is released by the weekend, the hijackers will blow up our plane. Like we could forget. He says we all need to write to Ted Heath, the Prime Minister, and the hijackers will send our messages to him.

Apparently we have to be short and sweet. So I've put:

> *Please release Leila Khaled, imprisoned in London.*
> *I want to come home alive. Anna, aged 15.*

Tim is sitting next to me, looking at his piece of paper.
'I don't know what to write,' he says. 'Will you help me?'
'Of course.'
'The problem is, I don't really get what's happening...'
'It's complicated, isn't it?' I say. 'But we need the Prime Minister, Ted Heath, to save us, which he can, if he does what the hijackers say.'

'By letting that woman in London go?

'Exactly.'

'What happens if he won't?'

'I expect he will,' I lie. 'Especially if we write to ask him.'

But inside I doubt he can give in to kidnappers' demands. Don't politicians always say they won't?

'Do you think I should write in capitals?' Tim asks. 'Mr Garnett says my handwriting's hopeless.'

'I think a telegram comes out in capitals anyway, so do it however you like.'

'Oh, OK.' He starts to write. When he's finished, he holds it up for me to see. 'D'you think the Prime Minister will like it?'

PLEASE SAVE US I'M HUNGRY AND
SO IS FRED MY TERRAPIN. TIM XXX

'I think he'll love it.'

Rosemary comes to collect them. 'That's excellent, Tim,' she says. 'Let's hope it does the trick.' Tim looks pleased, then rushes off to finish his game with the twins.

Mr Newton is listening to the BBC World Service news on his transistor radio. He kept the volume down low at first, but the guards don't seem to mind. In fact they seem pleased to hear how much publicity they're getting. So now a crowd gathers around the Newtons' seats on the hour to listen to the news. I hear Big Ben strike. It reminds me of being in the kitchen at home. I wonder if Marni's listening? She always says that the World Service keeps her sane. Is it keeping her sane now?

I don't need to get up. I can hear it from here. They're talking about a thousand Red Cross meals waiting in Beirut to be transported to the three planes. Well, I wish they'd hurry up. I'm having stomach cramps a lot now and I've begun to feel dizzy whenever I stand up.

After the news, I slide down into the footwell to sleep, to pass time. But somehow it's more claustrophobic down here now. The bleak forest of black metal seat legs seem more firmly bolted to the floor. Why can't they move, let me have more space instead of barring me in? But they're not going anywhere. Like me.

Forget the seat legs, I say to myself. Close your eyes. Think of something else. I squeeze my eyes shut and think of the windows, the long line of windows down each side of the plane. But even they feel like a cruel illusion, trick windows that pretend you can look out on the world, but don't let you see out properly. They're too high up and too small. And what's out there anyway? A line of hills – and those tanks.

I give up trying to sleep and climb up onto my seat – only to feel barricaded in by the rows and rows of seats. Are they deliberately obscuring my view, like the passengers standing up all round the cabin? I'm desperate for space. I want to look a long way but I'm stuck inside this arch, this tunnel, with too many people squeezing themselves between lines of fixed chairs, between obstacles, turning sideways to pass one another, turning back to pass forward, up and down, up and down the narrow aisle.

And I'm losing any sense of the outside of the plane too, of its nose and its wings and its tail. I try to picture the tail rising majestically behind us, the strange VC10 tail with the engines at the back, but I can't see it. I know the body of the plane is huge, but the space inside seems fragmented into tiny suffocating little compartments. Compartments that I need to escape.

Now.

23

15.00 hrs

Hundreds of miles away in the same desert, and under the same murderous sun, the wind gets up. At first, there are just small flurries and sharp scatterings, but soon the sand is being whipped several feet above the ground. And, as the wind builds in strength, huge clouds billow up, armed with billions of stinging grains, and the desert begins to shift.

The ferocious wall of sand fills the sky, growing higher and higher, until it curls over at the top like a gigantic wave. The blood-red tsunami of sand, now many miles wide, gains momentum and races across the desert towards the plane.

There's little warning.

The sky darkens, and within seconds the storm blots out the sun and plunges the desert into darkness.

The sandstorm bombards the plane, slamming down on it, pounding the windows.

Clouds of red sand pour in through the open door. The clouds thicken, twisting and rolling down the cabin...

I hear cries, violent coughing and shouts as the crew and hijackers struggle to shut the door.

My eyes are stinging. I blink furiously, trying to wash the grit out, but the air is thick with it.

I can't breathe, can't see.

Rosemary runs past. 'Cover your face! Hold anything – blankets, *anything* – up over your nose and mouth!'

I grab my blanket and hold it over my face, see David and Tim doing the same. Then I duck my head down, crouch over.

But I'm suffocating. *Breathe, just a little.* There's no air.

I hear moaning and begin to panic. But then remember Marni's mantra: 'Breathe slowly, in through your nose, out through your mouth.' The blanket smells musty, of old earth.

Breathe. In.

The wind tears at the plane, buffeting it violently.

Out.

I feel it sway, move like it's a living thing.

Breathe in. There's the heavy clunk of the door being pulled to.

Breathe out.

How can the plane stand up to this?

Breathe in.

How long will it last? I sit hunched, while the wind screams and the rampaging storm thunders outside. I imagine the sand covering the wheels, rising up over the guerrillas in their trenches. Will it bury us alive? Entire villages disappear sometimes.

Slowly, slowly, the clouds of sand inside the plane settle a little. The air clears a bit more. People come out from under their blankets and scarves, their jumpers and coats.

I try to swallow, but my throat is too dry, bloated and thick. I try not to rub my grit-filled eyes and blink instead. But I'm so dehydrated I can hardly make any tears. Slowly though, they clear enough for me to see that every inch of everything – the seats, the carpets, the overhead lockers, the pleats in the curtains – is coated in a fine layer of red sand. David and Tim are outlined too. A red film covers their hair, their eyebrows, their eyelashes. It lies in every crease of their faces and necks. I wipe it from my ears. It's under my fingernails, in between my toes.

Everyone is wiping their eyes, coughing, brushing themselves down. I sweep the sand off my tray. A little trickles into my empty shoes, set together on the floor. How far had it come? From North Africa? From Bahrain? They say the sands of the Sahara sometimes fall on southern France.

Eventually the storm outside abates, and when they open the door again, I add my name to the captain's list for a turn to look out, to breathe fresh air.

We all carry on clearing up. Someone is complaining about the sand in their whisky. Tim's gathering it up to wear like soft red war paint.

'I'll look just like a Kalahari caveman,' he says, smearing it onto his sticky forehead.

When I finally get my turn at the open door, there's a new world outside. Our little piece of desert has changed. The softer sand beyond the trenches and the hard flat-topped hillocks have disappeared beneath a magnificently ridged dune rippling away into the distance.

So, I think, it really is a land of shifting sands, a place without maps, where everything keeps moving.

And nothing remains the same.

24

16.00 hrs

I'm standing in the doorway when Mr Newton lumbers into view, his trousers hitched up a little too high as usual. He staggers towards me from the aisle, still etched in red sand, sways briefly beside me, before collapsing down onto the black crew seat.

He's been drinking steadily all day. I can smell the alcohol fumes, and his sour sweat.

He leans forward and fixes his tired eyes on me. 'Now, little lady,' he says, slurring his words and throwing one arm out as if he's trying to get rid of it, 'come and sit here, next to me.' He blinks and pats the seat next to him.

'I'm OK, thanks, Mr Newton,' I say.

'That bastard Prime Minister going to save us, you think?' Thick saliva gathers at the corners of his mouth as he speaks. To my relief, he doesn't wait for a reply but pulls a packet of cigarettes out of his top pocket, lights one with a trembling hand and takes a long drag.

He peers up at me again, his eyes bleary. 'What d'you say your name was?'

'Anna.'

'Ah.' The ash on his cigarette glows and lengthens. 'Last days on earth, you know.' He takes another drag. A small hollow tube of ash falls, breaks up on his dark trousers. 'I'm tired,' he says, staggering to his feet and lurching towards the open door.

'Mr Newton!' I catch him by the arm and look around for help. But no one's paying us any attention. 'I'm . . . I'm going back now, Mr Newton. Why don't you come with me?'

He nods sagely, as if he understands everything there is to know. Then his mouth droops, his face crumples and two tears slide down his red-veined cheeks.

A hand reaches out and takes his elbow. The Giant.

'Hey!' Mr Newton shakes him off.

The Giant glances at me, gives me a quick smile and stands firm. 'This way, please.' He nods towards the aisle.

Mr Newton sighs, shrugs and totters back to his seat.

I follow, and watch the Giant settle him down further back, then walk past me to resume his conversation with the captain and Jim. The boy with the ammo belt joins them from the back of the plane. He's almost as tall as the Giant, but leaner and more graceful. I wonder what they're so busy talking about.

I can see David and Tim right at the back of the plane by the galley, but I don't feel like joining them. Mr Newton may have been drunk, but what he said might still be true.

These might be my last two days on earth. I look at my watch. Teatime. Whatever that means.

25

16.30 hrs

Sweaty's at the front, guarding the doorway. He shifts, turns and glances down the cabin and I duck out of view, what Dad calls 'keeping your head below the parapet.' He's always said, 'In difficult circumstances, don't attract attention.'

But I'm getting sick of pretending I don't exist.

Maybe I won't exist soon.

How will I die? Be shot, or blown up? I wonder which is the least painful? If you die a violent death, don't you become a ghost, stalking the earth for eternity? Imagine.

Unseen. Alone. For ever.

The pit of my stomach clenches. Alarm blossoms. It blooms and darkens, like ink in water.

I have to stop this. Stop this fear from spreading, from taking over.

I try to concentrate on Rosemary, walking past on her way to the front; on the two blonde girls making their way noisily to the back; on the redhead in first class that the bald man calls Maria. She's leaning provocatively against the bulwark chatting to Sweaty; on Mrs Green, fixing a pink ribbon to her daughter's head. I watch them all – and I see them as they really are: despite the calm, the smiles and bravado, they're all tense, terrified of dying.

They're holding on, like me; mothers for their children, men for their wives, the captain for his crew, the crew for the passengers.

How long can we all keep it up? And who am I holding on for? For Tim? For my family? For myself?

What if Mark and Sam were here too, as they could so easily have been? I think of the freckles on Mark's nose, the tension in his small muscular body. I remember his kindness and deep sense of loyalty. He's fire and restlessness too, and endless energy, always flitting from one activity to the next, easily bored, pacing, impatient... He'd hate it in here, all cooped up.

And then there's little, thoughtful Sam, always in his own world. I love the way he slips his small warm hand in mine whenever we cross the road together. I think about his silky brown hair, streaked by the sun, his little white shorts, his incredible ease underwater, where he seems happiest. Sam is an underwater seal, and Mark a bright impatient flame. Fire and water. I'd never realised that before...

Suddenly Mr Newton turns his radio up to full volume. People call, shout out, complain.

But I'm glad. It's distracting.

'*Mr Gary Sobers, the West Indian cricket captain, who has been described as the world's greatest cricketing all-rounder, was welcomed in Salisbury, Rhodesia, yesterday. Despite sanctions being in place...*'

Above it, I can hear Rosemary persuading Mr Newton to turn the volume down. It goes suddenly quiet, and in the lull I hear Tim's high-pitched voice talking excitedly to David at the back.

I decide to get up and see what they're up to.

David has his face squashed up against the porthole in the back door, looking out with one eye, his nose flattened against the glass.

'What *are* you doing?' I ask.

He turns. 'They're fixing what look like explosives to the wheels.'

'What?'

'Look,' says Tim. 'Bundles of them.'

I squint down. Sure enough, I can just see the edges of the bundles, tied with black tape, bunched around the back wheels. They're turning the whole plane into one enormous bomb.

And we're inside it.

David grimaces at me, then glances pointedly at Tim.

'Let's go and see if they've put some under the belly.' Tim is eager. 'We might be able to see from the front doorway.' He trots off up the aisle.

'David, you shouldn't encourage him,' I say. 'He just doesn't understand.'

'I haven't.'

Tim is back. 'Come on,' he says. 'Mr Newton's just given me a box of matches, says we should light one and flick it down next time Sweaty takes a leak against the wheel.'

David shrugs helplessly at me and follows Tim to the front.

I slump down, hugging my knees to my chest. I want to shut everything and everybody out.

'What are those two boys up to?' It's Rosemary.

I look up at her. 'They're checking the explosives.'

'Oh, they don't miss a thing, do they? I was hoping they wouldn't notice.' She looks more closely at me. 'They won't use them, you know.'

'If the British government doesn't let that hijacker go, they will,' I reply.

Rosemary squats down next to me. 'Anna, they'll work something out. There's still time. Try not to dwell on it. Now – ' she stands back up – 'I'm reminding everyone that as well as taking walks up and down the plane, you need to exercise your eyes by focusing them on the horizon. Everything in here's too close up. OK?'

'Mmm,' I say.

'You seem low.'

'Just want to get out.'

'I know. It's really hard. We're trying to persuade them to let us get to our luggage soon. Several people are running low on medication and need to get supplies from their cases. Come on.' She holds her hands out and pulls me to my feet. 'Let's see if the food's arrived.'

I follow her to the front.

'They've not just rigged the cockpit and flight deck with dynamite . . .' Jim starts saying to Rosemary as she approaches, before noticing me behind and wincing.

'She's already seen the explosives outside,' Rosemary says.

'Ah,' he says. 'Och, well, it's not all doom and gloom, Anna. They've agreed to us having another breather outside later on.'

I smile as if that's great news, but feel my hope running out.

26

17.15 hrs

The captain stands at the front. The Giant towers over him. It's odd, but there's something about his size and presence that seems to calm things.

'Would everyone sit down for a moment, please,' the captain calls. 'I have something good to tell you for a change. We've negotiated with the hijackers to allow us access to our luggage.' There's a murmur of delight. Tim looks across at me and does a joyful thumbs-up.

'They've agreed to let us go down in groups of ten at a time,' continues the captain, 'to pick out our own cases, open them and take out one or two items. They'll check when you've chosen them. Obviously some of you will want to take out much-needed medicines or toiletries – I know that the bathrooms have run out of everything – others will want to collect a change of clothes. Please be co-operative. Think about what might make your stay here easier. We'll be carefully watched while we do this, and I advise everyone to stick absolutely to this agreement, to their rules. We don't want any trouble. I don't need to reiterate that we're at the centre of a very volatile situation, which we don't want to make worse. As some of you are in dire need of medical supplies, I am suggesting that we all agree to this offer?' There are murmurs of agreement and a smattering of *Hear, hears*.

'What about those Red Cross meals they keep promising?' Mrs Newton calls out. 'We haven't eaten since this time yesterday.'

'Apparently they're still stuck in Beirut,' replies the captain. 'And I have no news about when they'll get here. I'll let you know if I hear anything. I've negotiated a little bread and water for us all this evening. If everything goes smoothly with the luggage, we may very well get it.' The captain turns to the Giant and says something. The Giant smiles a long, slow smile, then claps the captain lightly on the back.

The names of the first ten people to go down the ladder are called out. They are those who need to get medication, and include Susan and Mrs Green, the bald man in first class for some reason – and, more bizarrely, Mr and Mrs Newton. Apparently Mrs Newton said she suffered from migraines. Hangovers more like.

Before the first group return, the second group assemble. They're mainly the crew and when they go it feels odd without them here. I don't like looking at their empty seats. They're always talking though practicalities, organising the door rota, trying to keep the loos clean, pressing for meals, for lanterns at night, discussing safety. The plane feels and sounds different with them all missing. It's eerie, like they've been taken out and . . .

A light flurry, a breeze comes in through the open door and down the central aisle. My turn soon.

'What are you going to get out, Anna?' David asks from across the aisle.

'I thought of a warm coat for the nights, but I'm desperate for a change of clothes too,' I say. 'I can't decide. With all this sweating and no washing, maybe it's a bit pointless.'

'What I'd give to dive into the Wardroom pool right now.'

'*You* went there?' I'm surprised.

'Yes, sometimes. Why?'

'I never saw you.'

'Expect you were too busy with some guy.'

I ignore this. 'Seems ages since I packed. I can't remember what's in my case. And it'll all be so crumpled.'

'I think the world might forgive you for looking a bit crumpled,' he says, 'when we're released.'

'You really think we'll get out?'

'Yes,' he says, not looking at me. And I don't know him well enough to know whether he means it or whether he's just being encouraging. I desperately want to believe him, but then he adds quietly, 'We have to think that, don't we?'

Tim is restless. He's standing already. 'I'm going to get my comics.'

'No clothes?' I say. 'You'll feel better in a pair of shorts. Then you won't have to keep asking Rosemary to cut the legs off your trousers.'

'Don't think I've got any shorts in there,' Tim says. 'Maybe a T-shirt then, and some tuck.'

'Tuck! You've got tuck in there?'

He nods.

'Then I'm your new best friend.' David gets up and puts an arm round him.

Tim smiles. 'It's only a tube of Polo mints.'

'*Only*. Polo mints!' David says.

'Do you think I should leave Fred here when I go down?' Tim asks.

'Just put him under your chair,' I suggest. 'He'll be OK there. I don't think anyone will take him.'

'And they wouldn't get far, would they?' says David.

'No, but...' Tim frowns.

'What?' I ask.

'That horrible lady...' says Tim.

'What about her?' I say. 'She won't come on board now, Tim. She only comes at night, *especially* at night – just to scare us. Stupid old witch.'

'Don't you mean Lady Macbeth?' says David.

'Who's that?' asks Tim.

'A cruel woman in one of Shakespeare's plays,' I say, and I'm relieved when the conversation's stopped by Sweaty coming to tell us we're in the next group.

It's great to be outside again. Someone puts their hands around my waist to help me down onto the truck. I'm a bit disconcerted to discover it's David and jump quickly down to the ground before him. Then I feel strangely exposed. For a moment, I'm the only hostage there.

We're herded under the belly, past the bundles of explosives taped to the wheels and all down the undercarriage. Around us the hot wind stirs up eddies of sand like tiny whirlwinds. We can see the two other planes properly from here. I still can't see any faces at the windows, but can clearly see the truck under each now, on the other side from us. They must have a door

127

open too. Their luggage is also piled up outside in the shade under the wing, but there's no one by it except a few guerrillas milling about. Suddenly I realise why it's been put outside. It's so that they can rig up explosives in the empty hold.

Seven or eight guerrillas who I haven't seen before are guarding our luggage. It's stacked in lines and small piles: large and small, soft and hard, black, brown, navy suitcases, school trunks circled by thick leather belts, a guitar case.

Sweaty shoves his gun in my back. I lurch away from him, frightened – and furious. How dare he? I make sure I walk well ahead of him.

But there's my case! I can see the edge of it, the dark green cloth with brown leather piping, chosen by Marni. It's worn and scratched by all the trips to and from school. I feel a surge of emotion, seeing her handwriting on the cream label. And suddenly I can see Marni's hands stroking the last jumper flat before closing the lid, and Dad's strong square hand picking it up by the leather handle, pulling it from the boot of the Peugeot.

David, about to open his case, glances round and, seeing my face, calls out, 'Are you OK?'

I nod. He takes a step towards me, but Sweaty pushes him roughly back.

'Really, I'm OK.'

'Tim,' David calls over Sweaty's head, 'what about you?

'I'm fine.' His clear voice comes from somewhere behind me.

When it's my turn, I step forward to undo my case. But the zip sticks. I feel a wave of panic. I'm overcome by an illogical desire to run. I don't want to be down here with Sweaty and all the strange guards watching me. I want to be back on the plane. I don't want to open it so that Sweaty can see my things. I don't want him looking in on my life. I don't want him to have anything to do with it.

But I fumble with the zip, get it moving again, take a deep breath, lift the lid and peep in. A lump comes to my throat. On top of the neatly folded clothes and all the textbooks that remained unopened all summer, Marni has packed her special beginning-of-term letter. I fight back tears. Marni's handwriting. The handwriting that *is* Marni, every bit of her: her warmth, her strength and the safety of her.

But I have to concentrate, not miss my chance. I raise a hand and brush the tears quickly away, not wanting Sweaty to notice. Could I slip the letter out too? What if they take it off me? Is it better to take it or leave it safely here for later? Will it be too much to bear? I pull out my school coat, a rust-coloured Aertex top, my toothbrush, toothpaste and a pot of Nivea cream – and there's the PFLP badge Samir gave me the night he showed me where he used to live in Palestine. I hide it inside my clenched fist.

'You, Anna,' Sweaty says, 'hurry!'

How dare he use my name? The bastard. I snatch up Marni's letter and stuff it into the folded Aertex top. I show him the coat, shirt, tooth things and cream. He nods. Then he takes them all from me.

27

17.45 hrs

'I keep,' Sweaty says. 'You go there.' He points to beyond the trenches around our plane, past some low scrubby bushes to where there's a semicircle of tiered boxes and crates, Jeeps and trucks. Several of the women hostages are already over there: Mrs Newton, Rosemary and Celia looking tense and out of place, the two blonde sisters pressed together, the sun reflecting off their silver bangles. Nearer to me, Mrs Green, holding several boxes of pills, is refusing to be separated from Susan, who stands desolately crying. Maria, now separated from the bald man and escorted by two guards, walks self-consciously towards the Jeeps, stopping to flick her hair from her face every few steps.

The male crew are already climbing back up the ladder under escort. The other men being herded back towards the plane are calling out to us or shouting at the guards. I see Tim and David stop on their way back to the plane, worry written across their faces. Mr Newton is arguing with one of the guerrillas.

'This is outrageous!' he shouts. 'You can't just take the women off like this! Mary! Come back! Come back here!'

It's going to kick off, I think, pressing the edge of the small metal shield-shaped badge deeper into the palm of my hand. Someone's going to get shot... Someone's going to die...

I stop walking, stand dead still. The guard urges me on, but I feel strange, otherworldly. Sounds become muffled. Everything slows down. I feel a long way off... distant... in a vacuum.

Quite alone.

It's so quiet.

Faces press against the windows, Sweaty's mouth moves, Mr Newton is taken away. They're nothing to do with me.

The Giant's huge hands are open. He's nodding. He wants me to do something. I don't know what. He looks like my father. His eyes. They're the same blue-grey colour as...

...as Dad's.

My face screws up, tears come. I stand there helpless as they stream down.

Rosemary, shading her eyes by the trucks, beckons to me.

I walk slowly towards her. Trembling. In a daze.

She puts an arm round me. 'It's all right. There's been a misunderstanding. We didn't realise what they meant. The hijackers just want us for their photo.'

'Wh—' No word comes.

'They're having a photo taken to remember the hijack. They want the women in it. We'll be fine.' But there's a faint patch of pink, like a rash, blooming on her neck.

More women arrive. They stand in loose groups, clumped round the first line of boxes. Maria stands slightly apart from the rest of us, pulling her shirt down and chatting to Sweaty.

She leans over and touches him on the shoulder and laughs. And I feel shocked. How can she bear to be near him? The two sisters in miniskirts look frightened, the younger one picks at her fingernails. Rosemary goes over to reassure them. She's bare-legged now and without make-up, her hair loose, her nail varnish chipped.

The sun beats down. The earth is baking underfoot. Sweat runs in rivulets down my spine, it drips from my temples. I can see faces peering out from our plane, watching through the sealed windows. The captain, Alan and Jim crowd around the open door.

Suddenly there are loud shouts in Arabic and a great noise, as about forty more guerrillas climb out of the trenches and stroll towards us, laughing and chatting.

So many! All believing in a common cause, believing this is the right thing to do – even if it means killing us.

They gather in the area in front of us, and when the Giant blows a whistle they start clambering onto the trucks and boxes behind.

The Giant asks Rosemary to place the women in among the guerrillas for the photo.

'Mrs Newton, would you go there?' she says. 'And, Celia, there.' She points. 'Maria, over there, and Anna, up there.' We go off singly, and are helped up onto the boxes by the men.

I'm handed up high onto the bed of a big truck to join a group of guerrillas who seem to be behaving as if they are on holiday. They move aside to give me space. I stand stiffly among them, not understanding what they're saying, and uncomfortably far from Rosemary and the others.

The sun, now low in the sky, casts a warm golden glow over the whole scene. Suddenly, from the left horizon, a white van, flanked by two Jeeps with gun emplacements, comes over the top of the escarpment and tears down, trailing a cloud of dust. As it draws up in front of us, the men whoop and whistle and cheer.

From the van steps a small round Arab with a short pointed beard, wearing a white *thawb* and a black headband with a red-and-white head shawl tucked in around it. He starts taking equipment out of the van and assembling it with great efficiency.

A tripod – and a tube. A gun? I feel a ripple of fear.

No, it really is a camera. We really are having our picture taken. And it feels suddenly so familiar. Of course! It's just like we're having a school photo.

How absurd! Laughter bubbles up inside – or is it hysteria? I look around at the men. They're just men, somebody's brother, somebody's father, someone's uncle. I begin to relax. They're refugees. They're homeless. They're men with a cause. Something I've never had. How feeble is that? And I smile at myself, and soften, and when I look up again, the men nearest to me smile back, their eyes friendly and full of humour.

They're OK. It comes as a shock. Are these men prepared to kill me? Really? The man next to me nudges me and points. A large bird of prey flies across the sky in front of us and above the plane, its shadow distorting over the wings. The bird soars and swings west against the great ball of the sun, flaps a little and turns, rising on a thermal, up and up until it's just a tiny speck.

I imagine it looking down from up there at the three white planes reflecting the quiet pink of the evening sky, surrounded by the distant black pinpoints of tanks. And us, ranged on the arc of Jeeps, the men in camouflage gear and the women among them, soft dots of colour.

'*Whahed, ithnain...*' the tall photographer shouts. The smiling men put their arms around each other's shoulders and around mine. I feel the weight of them, of their homelessness.

'*Thalatha!*' roar the men. The camera flashes.

And I'm sure all of us are smiling.

28

18.25 hrs

As the guerrillas help us down from the trucks, the sun begins to set, turning the desert apricot, orange, then red. Some of them come over to thank us. *Shukran*, they say, shaking our hands, holding them between theirs, patting us on the back. Then they point us back towards the plane.

I'm dazed, bewildered – relieved – happy. I feel the badge in my hand, glance quickly down at it, then hide it away again. Most of the others are ahead of me. I lag behind. I want to stay out here and watch the night set in, watch the darkness travel across the sand, watch the desert come alive with scorpions scuttling from under rocks, sidewinder snakes slithering from under the sand, toads and foxes emerging from underground hiding places.

I want to stay to ask the men what all this means to them, why they have to do this. I want to understand, to talk, to find out and make sense of it all. I don't want to go back into the plane. I want to stay out here, to breathe the cool night air.

A full moon rises behind the plane, golden as egg yolk; its crater face, wide-eyed and innocent, looks like there's nothing wrong with the world.

Someone touches me gently on my shoulder. 'You must go in.' It's the ammo-belt boy.

I don't move but stare up at him.

'You must go back in,' he insists, 'before . . .'

He speaks English. Why didn't he say something before? 'I must go in – before what?' I ask.

'Quickly.' He speaks quietly, walking by my side, his head down, encouraging me on. 'The second-in-command is coming.'

I feel a frisson of fear. The woman? Lady Macbeth?

'Where did you learn English?' I ask quickly.

'My mother . . .'

'Your mother?'

'Shhhh!' he falls silent as Sweaty and Maria overtake us.

'What's your name?' I ask quickly.

'Jamal.'

I walk under the plane to where the other women are queuing to climb the ladder, and my heart sinks when I see it's Sweaty helping us up. When my time comes, I feel his paws on my back, sense his animal smell – but then I'm distracted.

I can hear music.

29

18.30 hrs

The music floats on the air and the night is suddenly full of colour. It drifts up the aisle towards me as I enter the plane. I can't see who is playing at first, so I climb up onto my seat. Jim is sitting halfway down, surrounded by passengers, the guitar he collected from his luggage resting in his lap. He's strumming a song. Everyone is silent, listening. Then he starts to sing.

It's a song I know well. Everyone's been playing it all summer. 'Bridge over Troubled Water'.

Someone joins in. Then more and more people. At first I feel shy. Then, carried by the crowd of voices, I sing along too. My voice feels dry and rusty, but it soon gets stronger – and singing seems to lift something inside me: my body relaxes. I look around at the others, at their mouths working, at their glistening eyes. They look ordinary. They look happy.

CRACK! I swivel round.

CRACK! Lady Macbeth slams her hand down on the bulkhead at the front a second time.

The singing stutters to a halt. There's a final chord from Jim, then silence.

'Who said you could sing?' She marches down the aisle, her eyes blazing. Passengers retreat back into the empty seats, like reef fish hiding from a shark.

She stands over Jim, who remains in his place.

'GET UP!'

He stands slowly and faces her. 'Is something wrong?' he says calmly. Lady Macbeth flips her pistol from its belt casing. Her eyes brim with hatred as she clicks the safety catch off and levels it at his head.

She holds out her other hand for the guitar.

He passes it to her. 'I take it you don't like my playing then.'

She doesn't move. Jim closes his eyes, drops his head.

I stop breathing. Wait for the shot.

But she lowers the gun, turns on her heel and walks back up the aisle.

I watch her pass, then breathe again. She stands opposite the open door where we can see her, raises her arm and slams the guitar down. There's a crack of split wood and the dissonant tremble of strings as it hits the ground. Then we hear the ladder creak as she climbs down into the night.

A terrible silence follows, the silence of disbelief and shock.

But then I hear it, coming from the back of the plane. The small voice wobbles a little at first, but then picks up. It's a beautiful voice, high and pure. It's Tim's.

He's singing the chorus again and the words ring out, loud and clear.

Everyone joins in.

The song wafts through the open door and spills out into the night.

30

19.00 hrs

'Tim!' I cry. 'You were amazing! I didn't know you could sing like that!'

David claps him on the shoulder. '*You're* a dark horse. You never let on. Are you a chorister?'

Tim nods, grinning up at us. 'I sing every day, and at all the cathedral services on Sundays...'

The captain, Jim and Rosemary come over to congratulate him.

'Blimey,' I say quietly to David. 'D'you think the younger you are, the less scared you feel?'

'It's probably easier,' David says, watching the captain shake Tim's hand, 'when you can't imagine the consequences.'

'He doesn't really believe anything can happen to him, does he?'

'No. He still thinks he's immortal.' David gives a short laugh. 'Must be nice.'

Tim turns back to us.

'You're crazy, Tim,' I say, smiling. 'Crazy as that terrapin.'

'Thanks,' Tim says. 'The twins are looking after him at the moment.'

'Hey, when are we getting that Polo mint?' David asks.

'Oh yes, here you are.' Tim takes half a packet out of his pocket.

'Where have they all gone?' I ask. 'You haven't given them all away, have you?'

'No, I swapped the twins one each for another go on their Slinky.' He tries to remember. 'And I gave Rosemary one and I've had three myself.' He offers us the packet.

'Are you sure, Tim?' I say, 'Shouldn't you . . . ?'

'Course he's sure,' David says, helping himself quickly to one and popping it in his mouth. He closes his eyes and sighs loudly.

Tim grins. He pushes the tube over to me. 'Go on.'

I can't resist. I put the mint in my mouth, stick my tongue in the hole, feel the words written on the side and savour the utter mintiness of it. 'Mmm,' I say. 'Wonderful! It actually feels like I've brushed my teeth!'

'Mmm,' David mimics me. 'Fresh breath at last.' He pushes his mint out and holds it between his teeth. 'Argh, it's getting thinner.'

I'm just silent with the delight of it. Before I can thank Tim again, he's off to check on Fred.

David pushes the mint to the side of his mouth. 'Enjoy your photo with the guerrillas?'

'Not entirely,' I reply. 'David, did you know Sweaty confiscated all the stuff from my case?'

'No, it's all back on your old seat,' he says. 'At least, I assumed those were your things.'

And there they are: the clean shirt, my toothbrush, toothpaste and Nivea cream, and Marni's letter too. It's like Christmas all over again!

While my Polo mint melts into the thinnest wedding ring, then cracks in half and disappears, I hide the unopened letter and my PFLP badge in my shoes and push them under my seat. Maybe I'll show the badge to the boys later. I'm desperate to read Marni's letter, but I want to do it in private.

In private. What am I saying? It's worse than boarding school here. The only place that's completely private is the toilet, which is not a nice place to spend any time in at all; it smells so awful. So I leave the letter for later, when I'll probably *really* need it, and go to the toilet to change as quickly as I can into my clean clothes.

First I take some tissues and clean myself, not with water but with my Nivea cream. Then I change my clothes. By the time I get back to my seat, I feel like a completely new person – freshly dressed and much *cleaner*. Shame about my hair...

David and Tim are taking bets on whether the Red Cross meals will arrive in time for supper. But when supper does finally arrive, it isn't a tantalising three-course meal but a grim little cup of salty water. It's quite revolting, but I manage to drink it somehow. I suppose I'm trying to set a good example to Tim, but he screws up his face and closes his mouth firmly.

'That is gross!' he says. 'And I can't do it.'

'Come on,' I say. 'We need the salt with all the sweating we're doing. Do you want to have cramps, or will you knock it back and be brave?'

'Urrgh!' he cries, shuddering as he swallows it. 'Why can't we have ordinary water? That was *disgusting*.' Then he looks up at me and grins his pixie grin. 'Time for another Polo mint, I think.'

I smile. 'But how many have you got left?'

'Well, actually only two now.'

'Oh, Tim! They went fast.'

'I know.' He pops one into his mouth, hesitates and turns to me. 'Would you like...'

'Oh no.' I feel desperate as I say it. 'You keep that one for yourself. You've been far too generous already.'

And just when I'm feeling as empty as I think it's possible to be, Rosemary comes round with a tray of unleavened bread! We each take a small piece. I look at it and saliva rushes into my mouth. It has a soft white frayed edge like a torn cloud, is golden on top and has charcoal griddle lines underneath. I tear off a tiny piece, smell the mouth-watering aroma of fresh bread first and then put it in my mouth. I chew, savouring the subtle floury oil taste, then swallow and feel my digestive juices rising in delight.

Forget steak and chips, ice cream or Rosemary's mother's sherry trifle, this piece of bread is the best thing ever. It's *so* delicious, *so* intense – but it's gone in a flash.

And my stomach craves it all over again.

31

19.50 hrs

With the scrap of food and the cool night air causing a welcome drop in temperature, the mood on board seems to change. We breathe more easily, feel more active, now that the exhausting heat has gone. I tidy my seat pockets, go through my bag and then decide to take another walk up and down.

The hurricane lamps cast their warm yellow glow. People are smoking, conversing, exchanging ideas and even addresses – all washed down with the last of the duty-free alcohol.

I stop by Tim and the twins, who are comparing their Junior Jet Club logbooks. They've all taken off their *Unaccompanied Child* badges and pinned on their Junior Jet Club ones. Their little navy logbooks are spread open on their tables. Several pages of logged flights are filled in, and they're reading their columns out loud in turn, comparing dates, arrival and departure times and studying the scribbled signatures of different captains.

'The best bit about flying,' Tim says, 'is being allowed to visit the cockpit.'

The twins nod their identically tousled heads.

'I'm nearly at the special certificate,' he says to me. 'You have to fly 50,000 miles with BOAC for that.' He leans over to me and whispers, 'The twins aren't quite there yet.' Then he continues, 'It's really annoying though, because we need to log this flight, but it's stuck on the ground.'

'Well, we may not always be,' I say. 'And then I'm sure they'll count it.'

'The twins are lending me their Slinky later,' he says. 'We're going to ask the Giant if we can see if it'll flip down the wooden ladder.' I leave them discussing this and wander back towards David.

He's reading one of Tim's comics. He says he's just been to the front to try to talk to the blonde sisters, but they made it quite clear they weren't interested, by half ignoring him and going on about the *much* older guys they knew and their incredibly flash cars.

'Serves you right,' I say, secretly pleased – not that I fancy him, of course. 'They're *way* out of your league.' He looks at me morosely.

I leave him in the doldrums, and walk up the plane, beginning to feel restless again. I squeeze past Mrs Newton trying to cadge a last drink off Alan and Celia, who are sipping gin, by the look of it. Alan leans forward, his elbow crooked, his hand on his thigh, pretending to listen intently to Mrs Newton's request, occasionally running his hand through his hair, as if to reassure himself it's still there. The captain and Jim, nursing whiskies, sit nearby, looking amused.

On my way back I stop by the emergency door about two thirds of the way down. I can see the wing quite clearly from here. And there's the moon! It's wonderful: huge, smooth and silvery calm, my connection to the outside world, to all the space and air out there. It quietens me somehow, so I stay moon-bathing for a while.

Then I go back to pacing the wing from the aisle. Eight big paces, so very wide. No wonder you walk over it to get off in an emergency. There's a high ridge running across the wide backward slope, and I can see the edges of the three flaps on the top surface, the ones that flip up to slow you down when you're about to land. I wonder what the pointed bits sticking out under the wing are for, maybe to help the wind fly over it? Wasn't that what we learned in physics, that the wind travelling over the wing was what causes a plane to take off? That wing flew me. Wants to fly me again.

A small group crowds around Mr Newton's radio to listen to the evening news. I stop too.

'*The head of the International Red Cross Mission in the Middle East yesterday denied that the Palestinians were subjecting their skyjacked hostages to "mental and psychological torture". Speaking from Amman, he said that the guerrillas had a "very friendly and humane attitude. However," he said, "there are reports of the children being taught war songs and being given automatic weapons to play with."'*

Where on earth did they get that from? I wonder. Do they just make things up, or is that what's happening on one of the other planes?

I give up on the news and walk the plane some more, discovering that there are exactly fifteen strides from my seat through first class to the open front door. One for every year of my life. I pass Rosemary playing peep-bo with the baby in the carrycot, who breaks into peals of giggles every time she reveals her face. Further back, Mrs Green has her arm round Susan's thin shoulders. She's wearing a new dress and is wrapped in her mother's blue cardigan.

There's a conversation about films going on between the two blonde sisters and Maria. They all have glasses of booze in their hands and are smoking. Maria has wide-set eyes and a slightly disgruntled expression. She must be about their age, eighteen or nineteen, but the other two seem to be only just tolerating her. She tilts her head to one side as she listens, appearing to agree with everything they say.

When I'm back sitting down, Tim and the twins file past. 'We've decided to ask the captain,' Tim says, 'if he'll sign our Junior Jet Club logbooks, even though we haven't arrived in England yet.'

'Good luck,' I say. 'I hope it works.'

'May I join you, your ladyship?' David says, before sliding down beside me.

'For you, sir – anything.'

'You are too gracious.' But then, without warning, he's serious. 'That was awful, seeing you all taken off this afternoon for the photo. Not knowing what was going on.'

'No, it wasn't good.'

'I thought they were going to shoot you or something.' He smiles suddenly. 'Be odd without you there across the aisle.'

'Well, you may have to put up with me here for a little longer,' I say lightly. 'There's not much chance of a change in the seating plan.'

'It's funny, isn't it?' he says. 'You and I are in a kind of limbo here. We don't get included in all the adult stuff going on in first class, because we're not counted as adults, but we're not looked after like the younger children either. Basically we're *not* seen *and* we're not heard.'

'I know,' I commiserate. 'And we weren't even given a children's colouring pack to play with.'

'Exactly. It's not fair. I feel like drawing the first-class curtain on the whole lot of them.'

'You know what?' I sigh dramatically. 'We'll just have to grow up.'

'I am *trying*,' he replies. 'Do you think if I keep wandering through the adult zone, something might rub off on me?'

'Unlikely,' I say, 'but give it a go.'

He gets up and I watch him walk through first class towards the open doorway. Sweaty leans against the cockpit door. 'No!' he shouts, waving his gun at David. 'Back! Go back!'

David faces Sweaty, his fists clenched, looking as though he'd like to hit him hard in the face. Instead he turns and walks back down the aisle.

I don't want him to know I've witnessed that, so I open *Wuthering Heights* and force myself to focus on it. Read properly, I say to myself. Hear the words in your head. Get absorbed. It'll take you away from here.

'*As it spoke, I discerned, obscurely, a child's face looking through the window. Terror made me cruel; and, finding it useless to attempt shaking the creature off, I pulled its wrist onto the broken pane, and rubbed it to and fro till the blood ran down and soaked the bedclothes.*'

How cruel!

Why is everyone so *cruel?* Sweaty, Lady Macbeth.

What if I witness something awful here, something really

awful, happening to any one of these living, breathing people?
I'll never escape the memory of it, will I, even if I do survive.

It'll be etched on my brain for ever.

I need Marni's letter.

I need it now.

I reach down and take it from my shoe, open the envelope
and smooth the page out.

My darling Anna,

*By now you'll be safely back at school (without any hitches,
I hope). I imagine you've unpacked your case, with your
friends all about you, swapping tales of the summer.*

*The boys are about to fly back, and then Dad and I will
be home by the end of the week. What an extraordinary
thought. At least we'll all be in the same country for a
change. How good that will be!*

*By the time you come home, there'll be a lovely (I
promise) newly painted (ditto) room all ready for you; the
walls that blue you mentioned. As soon as I see the new
house, I'll give you the lowdown on it. Let's hope we get
a decent bit of a garden this time.*

*Enjoy your term, my treasure. I know you will. Work
hard, play hard – and wear those new shoes with pride!
I'll call you on Sunday, as usual. Until then, my precious
girl, missing you and loving you to distraction,*

Marni xxx

I hear Marni's voice and feel calm again. It was written to
me, just to me, and I feel the power of that. I run my eyes over
the familiar curves and flourishes of her strong handwriting:
the firmly crossed *t*s, the purposeful uprights, straight as her

back, and the running rush of her final signature, as if it isn't herself she cares about at all.

I see her sitting at the kitchen table, where she writes every week to her sisters, my aunts, Birdie in Cornwall and Diana in north London. She's concentrating, with a slightly clenched jaw and pursed lip, and the finger she's guiding the pen with has a skewed nail that got stuck in the laundry mangle when she was a child. I bury my face in that letter and quietly sob.

32

Bahrain - 22.00 hrs

Marni is leaving Bahrain on another plane, carrying her and the rest of the family home to the UK. It flies up over the southern tip of the island, away over the deserts of Saudi Arabia, high above the fuselage of Anna's plane thousands of feet below.

Inside it, Marni, with her two boys slumped on either side, sits awake, thinking of her missing child. Her precious girl, all on her own.

And even though Marni doesn't exactly believe in God, she prays to whatever or whoever is the fount of all goodness. She prays, as she has never prayed before, that her daughter is still alive. Then she prays for strength to face the days to come. And though she draws some comfort from it, fear still rages in her chest. She thinks of her own mother, of the prayer she said every night, printed on a yellowing card decorated with faded flowers. Something about *the shadows lengthening, the busy world being hushed, the fever of life being over . . .* What words.

That was it. *Grant us a safe lodging and peace at the last.* And the ancient words pour oil on her turmoil.

She repeats them to herself and breathes more quietly, grateful for the time to think, to process the terrible day. And, as she does so, image after image rises up. Of Anna by Lake Naivasha in Kenya, in a drooping nappy on a lawn strewn with red hibiscus flowers. As a toddler, sitting on the high wooden bed in Hong Kong with the black mamba snake hissing under it, sitting obediently, so quiet and still, while Marni slammed the wooden bar down and down on its head. She smiles, thinking of Anna's hopeless expression, having stitched her blue school dress to her sampler, and how the chlorine in the pool in Aden turned her blonde hair a fluorescent green. She sees her on the farm in Cornwall at her grandfather's feet, learning to whistle through new front teeth. And she thinks of her in water, always in water – swimming, diving and water-skiing – and on that last day on the roof and when they went shoe shopping. Is she wearing them now?

Anna, my darling girl, I'm here. I'm here with you.

Outside the window she sees the blurred moon.

Can you see it too, Anna ?

Can you? Are you looking?

The night wears on. The plane flies over the smooth Mediterranean Sea, over the snow-capped Alps, over the fields of France to the small island lying on the edge of Europe.

As dawn breaks, Marni looks down at the fields and hedgerows, at the glinting reservoirs, at the cows and the sheep, at the extraordinary greenness of it all. And when she sees the roads silvered by recent rain, and the light trails of traffic on the ring road, she weeps to be home.

33

Revolutionary Airstrip, Jordan – 22.00 hrs

Just after the lamps are turned low, David and I watch Maria putting on her pink lipstick, straightening her dress and then sneaking off down the plane. We watch her disappear into the dark, where we can see Sweaty's torch flickering.

I'm amazed, horrified. 'She was flirting with him earlier,' I say. 'It was gross. She's mad, going back there on her own.'

'Right under everyone's noses,' David says, incredulous. 'And what on earth does she see in Sweaty?'

'Not much in the dark,' I say. 'Maybe that helps.'

'You know she told Tim that she doesn't speak a word of Arabic.'

'I doubt if they're conversing.' I smile.

He laughs quietly, then shakes his head. 'Does she really think that flirting with him will keep her alive? Make him save her? Mark my words, it'll end in tears...' I like him saying that. It reminds me of Dad.

Mr Newton's radio, which has been burbling on low, suddenly rises in volume. It's the news. Apparently President Nixon is ordering a task force from the US fleet in the Mediterranean to within striking distance of Jordan. The newscaster says Nixon is thinking of sending in the Marines, but is considering whether it might endanger our lives.

'God, slight understatement,' David says.

'For Christ's sake, turn that thing off and let us sleep!' someone shouts.

'Are you crazy?' someone shouts back. 'Don't you want to know what's happening out there?'

And that's when Lady Mac arrives, which quietens everyone, including the radio.

She raises her head as she enters, stares disdainfully at the captain and crew sitting in the front seats, then narrows her eyes to peer down the plane. She waits as Sweaty rushes up from the back, turning up the lamps as he goes. Her two guards stare blankly out at him. Why are the sleeves of her shirt rolled up? What does it mean?

There's a deathly hush and then she begins to pace, moving her head from side to side, like a snake, her eyes flat and opaque.

This time she hardly raises her voice. 'You are all going to die,' she says, and pauses. 'Detonators have been attached to the explosives, so now we can blow you up at the press of a button.' As she passes by, almost brushing my shoulder, I'm aware of the black hairs on her forearm, the small scar on her top lip. 'And if your Prime Minister doesn't do as we say, we will do it.' She raises her voice. 'The execution deadline is midday on Saturday. He has just thirty-eight hours to decide –' she pauses before continuing – 'and then we will either blow you up or shoot you one by one.'

I go numb. The captain gets to his feet. I stare fixedly at the place where his hair touches the top of his ear. 'I'd like to speak,' he says.

Her lips curl. 'I said sit down!' She nods at the guards and turns her back on him. He's pushed down in his seat at gunpoint.

She's wired and pacing again, coming this way.

And that's when I realise it. Her eyes, the windows to her soul, are dead.

Don't look! Don't look in there. I drop my head.

Marni! I think quickly. Marni, what are you and Dad and the boys doing right now? Where are you? I really need to see you, to speak to you. It's awful here, awful. I want to see you, to tell you . . . I'm still alive, Marni. I'm still . . . I'm OK, really I am, Marni. I'm still alive.

34

Friday 11th September 1970

03.00 hrs

I wake with a start in the middle of the night, when the first slivers of light are creeping into the plane. It's very cold, but I'm not freezing like last night, as I'm wrapped in my school coat as well as my blanket. I'm down in the footwell and David is asleep above, stretched across my three seats. I wonder how he got there. I didn't hear him arrive. Tim is fast asleep curled up under his blanket on the seats opposite.

I hear a strange noise from the back of the plane and raise my head to listen. My hips are numb from being pressed against the chair frame. My arm's still asleep. I rub it and feel the fizzing prickle of pins and needles. There it is again, a noise like someone moaning through a shut mouth. Is someone having a nightmare? And again. No, it's like a whimpering dog, soft and in pain.

'David,' I hiss, shaking him. He groans. 'David. Listen,' I whisper.

'What?'

'At the back.' We listen like guard dogs, our ears shifting every time there's the slightest creak. There's a muffled cry and scuffling, running footsteps, then Maria rushes past. People stir, turn over. Some shuffle to their feet, stretch and sit down again. One or two get up and use the toilets.

The captain stands briefly at the front, outlined by the grey light filtering through the doorway. He kneels down next to Maria, who's sobbing, heaving. He tries to quieten her, but the noise goes on and on. She's inconsolable.

'My God,' David says. 'What's happened to her? What's Sweaty done?' The sobbing subsides little by little. Silence of a sort streams back. I lie down, feeling a thick dread. Poor Maria, poor desperate Maria.

'Are you OK?' David asks. His hand reaches down, touches my shoulder covered by the blanket. He leaves it there and I find comfort in the warmth of it, in the soft pads of his fingers.

I stay awake for a long while, listening to his breathing gradually become regular. His hand loosens and slides off me as he fades into sleep.

My mind is calmer now. I think of the moon fading in the sky outside, the stars disappearing into the milkiness of dawn. I think of the day, the reporters, the luggage, the photo, the explosives, the song, the fags and booze and the wonderful piece of bread. I think about Tim's singing, but I refuse to think about Lady Mac; I refuse to let her in.

35

04.00 hrs

I'm dreaming, restless... *standing at the open back door...* *the night air is cold on my face. Someone below grabs my ankles,* *drags me out. I cry, fall. Down, down. Sweaty pushes me into the* *black moonless desert at gunpoint. I'm kneeling on the floor in* *a camouflaged tent. Lady Mac's eyes glitter. She jabs her finger* *at me. 'Whose fault is it that we have no land?' she shouts. 'Tell* *me! TELL ME!' She circles. 'You WILL tell me or you will DIE.'* *She grabs my ponytail, drags my head back and up, thrusts her* *face in at me, makes me look into her eyes. And all I see in there* *is my own death.*

I wake shaking, breathing in deep, ragged shudders.

'Anna. Anna.' Someone is patting my shoulder. I try to come to.

'You were crying out,' David says.

I'm alarmed. What have I said? 'Sorry,' I mumble.

'Sounded like you were calling for someone,' he says. 'Sounded like Marmite or something.'

'My mother. Marni,' I say. 'I call her Marni.' I like saying her name here.

'Marni,' he says. 'Why Marni?'

'From the sea. It means, from the sea.' I feel drugged.

'No – really?'

'Yes really. She's Cornish. I couldn't say Mummy when I was small. Marni stuck.'

I wipe my tears, breathe the night air and feel glad he's there.

36

11.30 hrs

It's mid-morning of the third day, the last full day for Ted Heath in London to decide our fate. What's he thinking? What's he going to do? Did our telegrams make *any* difference? What hope have we really got? No one here seems to want to talk about it any more, which makes me feel that we must be completely doomed. We're just a planeload of helpless hostages with our heads in the sand.

Hungry, thirsty, filthy, sweaty hostages. We've just heard that a woman in first class has been hoarding soaps and hand creams from the toilets. No wonder we ran out so quickly. No one's washed properly for days now. It seems an age since I tried cleaning myself with Nivea cream. The clean shirt against my skin made me feel brighter, more optimistic, but that was then. Now I wish I'd got out some clean underwear. I try convincing myself that I won't be here for ever – then I realise that has two meanings, two endings.

The toilets are unbearable again. It's gross knowing when you're in there that everything slides straight down into the open pit in the desert for everyone outside to see. With no water to flush anything down, the sewage only slides *slowly* out into the desert, and in the heat... the smell makes me gag. People have complained to the captain about it. But what's he supposed to do? I avoid going as long as I can, which is quite easy, since I hardly eat or drink anything now.

I woke this morning to the smell of sick, to the sounds of people straining and gagging, vomiting on empty stomachs. It's enough to set you off yourself. When it's happening I cover my ears and rock to and fro, humming. David says I look completely insane. Well, I will be if this continues much longer. And guess what? The baby at the front has started to whimper again. Sounds like he's revving up for something more substantial.

I'm getting really fed up of looking at the same stuff day after day: the rows of seat tops, the stiff little armrests, the seat pockets bulging with rubbish, the lines on the plastic ceiling, the coat shelves stuffed to overflowing. I'm fed up of the sign on the chairback telling me that my life jacket is under my seat. *I know*. And what possible use is it anyway? Hardly life-saving. It's just a pointless piece of canvas. I decide to pull it out. *Do not inflate in the cabin*, it says, and I immediately want to pull the cord just for the hell of it, and watch it puff up, fatten out. But I don't. There's little enough space already.

The day heats up.

Time passes, ticking on towards the deadline tomorrow. Talking about it is now actively discouraged. It's been consigned to the *unspoken zone*, the *no-point-in-speculating place*. And time seems to have drifted there too. No one is allowed to mention that either. There's no framework. No mealtimes. When Mr Newton's radio batteries died, the outside world went silent, abandoned us.

The plane itself is quieter too. It's horrendously hot. The midday sun beats down, searing through the windows. There's not an inch of breeze. Everyone is still; conserving energy, slowly melting. Except me. I'm rubbing Nivea into the filthy soles of my feet and trying to wipe them clean with a tissue. It's an impossible task, but it gives me something to do. I wonder whether I should ration the cream, but decide not to bother. What's the point? Tomorrow either we'll be freed, or...

I feel jumpiness like a fist in my throat, so I take Marni's letter out of my shoe and read it again while fanning myself with the envelope.

My treasure... my precious girl... Dad and I will be home by the end of the week... we'll all be in the same country... loving you to distraction... loving you to distraction...

It leaves me bereft. Each word a wound.

I fold it up but hesitate about sliding it back into my shoe. Since I've been wearing them barefoot, they've started to smell. I must have been mad flying in them; perfect chunky shoes for an English winter, but ridiculous in 140-degree heat. What I'd do for a pair of flip-flops. I tip the badge out from the toe, and shove the shoes back under my chair. Then I push the badge and Marni's letter right to the bottom of my bag.

Jamal, the ammo-belt boy who I spoke to yesterday, climbs on board. He glances down the aisle, then stands by the galley opposite the open doorway and lights a cigarette. The Giant stands a little way off, his gun resting against his leg.

Occasionally he picks it up and wanders around at the front, or up and down the aisle, before sitting down again.

I get up and walk into first class.

'Can I have a turn in the doorway soon?' I ask the captain.

'Sure.' He scans the list. 'After Mrs Newton.'

'How many before her?'

'Just four.'

I return to my seat.

David sits down beside me. 'It's funny,' he says. 'Wearing this clean shirt makes me feel I'm going to be stuck in here for longer.' He watches the Giant walking up and down the aisle. 'Why does he have to keep doing that?' he says irritably. 'It's not like we're going anywhere.'

'He's just checking...' But I can't be bothered to finish the sentence. It's too hot and I feel too bad-tempered.

'Oh, right, making sure we're not sneaking off one by one.'

'Yes,' I say, and then try to make more effort. 'Like in that movie where prisoners do gymnastics over a horse so that the others can dig a tunnel underneath and escape.'

'I see.' David looks at me as though I'm crazy. 'So he's checking for holes under the seats?'

'Exactly,' I reply. 'And he's missed Tim, who, as we speak, is swinging down to freedom on Mrs Newton's knotted tights.'

David smiles, then nods down at my feet. 'Given up wearing your shoes, I see.'

I make a face. 'They were smelling.' I look at his flip-flops. 'Wish I'd worn those.' He has nice feet. He's nice altogether, just a bit young. 'God,' I say, 'I'd do anything to wash my hair; it's full of sand.' It was so itchy this morning I put it up in two very tangled plaits.

'Mine too,' he says. 'Like the plaits though. Not bad for a dumb blonde.'

I raise my eyebrows. 'Have you come over here just to insult me?'

'No, I thought you might like to amuse me, for once.'

'*For once!* No pressure then.'

'Anna –' his voice changes, becomes serious – 'are you worrying about your folks?'

'Yes.'

'I really want mine to know I'm OK,' he says. 'You know, still alive.'

'Yes. But we were in those photos, David. Maybe they've seen you there.'

'Yeah.' He looks around. 'God, I feel so cooped up.' I'm silent. 'What shall we do now then?' he says. 'Recount the King of Jordan's tanks?'

I smile a little and sigh. 'You know we did that yesterday.'

He gives a short laugh. 'I know. But maybe there are more now.'

'That may not be a good thing for us – in the end.'

'*In the end*,' he says. And we go quiet, contemplating what that might mean.

'I've got something to show you,' I say, bending down and feeling around in the bottom of my bag for the badge. I hide it in my clenched fist and hold out my hand for him to guess.

He looks at it. 'Let me see – a mandarin. *Oh God, a mandarin!* Imagine peeling one, the smell, putting a segment in your mouth. It bursting open... the juice...'

'Stop!' I say. 'No, it isn't a mandarin.'

'Food or drink, by any chance?'

'Neither,' I say.

'Then I'm losing interest.'

'Close your eyes and put out your hand.' I place the badge on his open palm. 'OK.'

'What the...?' He looks at me, then back at the silver shield with the black inscription on it. '*P.F.L.P.*,' he reads, turning it over and over. 'Don't tell me, you've been one of them in the PFLP all along. No, wait, you were converted at the back of the plane by Sweaty.'

'Don't be disgusting,' I say. 'Have you seen Maria today?'

'Yes. She's keeping a low profile. Moved to the window seat and isn't really talking to anyone. Haven't seen Sweaty either, mind you. Perhaps he's got sacked.'

'That would be nice. Has anyone said anything?'

'What, to me? You must be joking. They're all pretending nothing's happened.' He looks down at the badge again. 'So how did you come by this? Are you *really* an undercover agent?'

'Yeah, definitely,' I say. Then, 'No, a friend, a Palestinian friend of our family in Bahrain, gave it to me a couple of days before I flew. Weird or what?'

'Weird. Anyway, it's obviously brought you immense good luck.'

'What, being hijacked?'

'You could look at it that way,' he says. 'But I expect you're feeling particularly fortunate about having met me.'

'Very funny,' I say, taking it off him. 'Actually, I think it's *going* to bring us immense good luck.'

'Oh, good! Go on, pin it on then.' He smiles. 'You'll cause a stir when they notice. They might even want to keep you.'

'No,' I say. 'I'm not wearing it. It's my lucky charm, my mascot, and it's going to remain a secret.' I look hard at him. 'OK?'

'OK,' he says solemnly.

And after that, somehow, against my better judgement, he persuades me to play cards – and I actually manage to win the first game.

'You know,' he says, dealing the next hand. 'Despite the incident with Sweaty and the ammo belt, you seem to be managing all this quite well.'

'I'm glad it looks like that,' I say, 'but what would you know?'

'Yeah, OK. But you seem quite self-contained.'

I shrug. 'Don't we have to be, if we go to boarding school? You learn to fend for yourself, don't you?'

'True.'

I watch Jamal at the front move aside to let Mrs Green and Susan nearer the open doorway. They're obviously anxious about the drop, as they stand well back holding hands, looking timidly out into the void.

'Moving around so often, every few years,' I say, 'makes you pretty adaptable, doesn't it?'

'Yeah.' He flips a card over. 'In the end it does. But sometimes it's painful getting there. I can remember going through a phase when I was about five of not being able to stay at kids' parties, having to leave the present and go straight home with Mum. I couldn't bear going into yet another room with all those kids I didn't know staring at me.'

'I bet you were sweet when you were five.'

'Course I was.' He turns and grins at me. There's the faint shadow of stubble growing on his chin.

'When I was five,' I say, 'my dad had to go abroad for months, and I was so upset that I started a "library" in my room – made up of little books stolen from school. Marni had to take them all back and apologise.'

'Blimey, thieving so young,' he says. 'But moving around so much does make you reliant on your own family, doesn't it, especially when you move to a new place and don't know anyone else. Me and my sisters and parents are incredibly close, really look after each other, even when we're apart. I'm really missing them.' He glances quickly at me to see my reaction and I try not to show how sad I feel. 'Anna,' he says, 'I haven't ever told anyone this, but whenever I meet someone I like, I immediately imagine what it will be like to say goodbye to them. You see, the only fixed things I have are my family and my friends at school.'

I nod. He's beaten me at cards again and starts collecting them in. 'At least going to boarding school teaches you to keep your feelings under control,' he says.

'You think that's a good thing?'

'Well, it helps in a situation like this.' He pushes the cards into their box.

I see that Mrs Newton is by the door. 'Look, David,' I say, nodding at her. She stands and turns her smoke-lined face up to the sun, drawing the air in dramatically, filling her lungs. Then she coughs and doubles over. 'It's my turn at the door next. I'm after her.'

'Hey! What about me?' he cries.

'I put my name down ages ago,' I say, getting up. 'I'll add yours now though if you like.'

'Oh, OK.' But he's clearly put out.

I go up and sit down on the black seat by the open door

and stare out. Jamal leans against the end cupboard, opposite the galley.

I glance quickly up at him. He's staring down the aisle. I can't get my head round it. He seems so normal, quite nice even, and yet he's actually prepared to kill us, to kill us all.

I want to understand what makes someone like him do something like this. I really do. And what have I got to lose?

In the end though, he comes over to me. 'Hello, Anna.'

'Hello.'

'Can I tell you something?' he says quietly. I turn to face him. 'You may choose not to listen, or not to believe me,' he says, his voice deep and reasonable, 'but, please, just for a moment?'

He sits down by me. It feels too close. I don't look at him.

'How can you do this?' It bursts out of me, brutally. 'How can you keep us here like this – like animals? How can you kill us just because you want publicity, for people to listen to you? Do you really think the world will have any sympathy for you if you kill us?' I'm surprised by my own vehemence. But I need to know. I stare angrily up at him.

'Please,' he says, looking straight at me, his eyes troubled, 'please, just listen.'

I nod curtly, and look out at the desert. He's gazing out too.

His voice is low and urgent. 'My brother and I grew up on a farm in orange groves. It had been in our family for hundreds of years. But the Israelis wanted the land, wanted to drive us from it.' He takes a deep breath. 'When I was eleven, we came home from school down the long straight track that led to the farmhouse. Our mother, then our father, ran out of the house. There was a burst of gunfire. They fell, face down. Dead. I dragged my brother into the long grass and we hid till it was dark. Then we left. We never went back. Couldn't.' He turns towards me. 'Tell me – where would you be if that had happened to you?' He looks right at me. 'Might you be here too?'

I can't answer him.

37

12.30 hrs

I get back from speaking with Jamal and find David and Tim sitting in my chairs trying to play whist despite the heat. I sit down and tell them the story of Jamal and his parents. They listen intently, David glancing up occasionally, Tim chewing his thumbnail.

'That's terrible,' Tim says at the end.

'He asked me what I'd do, if I were him,' I say.

'Well, I doubt you'd blow up a planeload of innocent people!' David says vehemently.

'No, but we've no idea what it must be like,' I say. 'And if the world won't listen, and you're going through so much . . . I mean, it's not that simple, is it?'

'S'pose not.' David isn't convinced. 'And you think he's telling the truth?'

'Yes, I do,' I say.

They finish their game.

Tim throws down his cards. 'I give up trying to win against

you.' He clambers across to the other side of the plane.

'What are you doing?' I call.

'Checking Fred.'

'You might let him win *sometime*,' I say to David.

'Yes, I should really,' he says. 'Though he is getting better.'

I watch Tim reach down and pull Fred's tin out from under his chair.

'He's gone!' he cries.

David and I stare across at him.

'I hid him up under there, behind my school blazer,' he says.

I clamber over to look. The tin's empty, but for a little water and a slop of brown weed.

'But, Tim, how?' I ask.

'He was getting too hot, so I left the lid off,' he says. 'Dad said I had to be careful . . .' Tears spill down his cheeks. 'He said I had to . . .' He starts to sob.

I put my arms around him. 'We'll find him. We really will. He can't have gone far. David, you ask the people in front and behind to look. See if they can see him. Tell them to be *careful*! I'll stay here and look under these chairs with Tim.'

'What if someone treads on him?' Tim wails. 'He'll be . . . !' He's really sobbing now.

David's still standing in the aisle. 'Shouldn't I help you look round here first?'

'We'll do that. Why don't you go and tell Rosemary and the captain as well? Quickly! Tell everyone on the way to be really careful where they walk.'

David disappears, watching the ground, stepping carefully.

The captain comes straight down to see Tim, looking concerned. 'How big's this terrapin, Tim?'

Tim holds out one little trembling hand. 'This big.' His voice is choked with emotion.

'OK, now, don't you worry. We'll find him. First we need to let everyone know he's lost.' He goes off down the cabin.

Tim wipes his eyes and we start searching very carefully around his seat and the ones behind and in front. We look in every nook and cranny, under every chair. We take down every tray and search in every magazine pocket.

But there's no sign of Fred.

38

13.15 hrs

We search the rest of the cabin. It takes ages. Everyone tries to help, but as the minutes go by, Tim becomes more and more distraught. In the end I have to take him back to his seat to calm him down. He's red-eyed and morose and cannot be comforted. As though, after everything else that's happened, losing his terrapin is the last straw. It's like he's shutting down. I talk quietly to him, telling him over and over how Fred couldn't have gone far, that he'll turn up eventually. Tim remains silent, then suddenly shudders into sobs again, as though all the grief in his small life is spilling out today, now, on this plane.

'Honestly, Tim,' I say for the umpteenth time, 'he'll be here *somewhere*.'

He looks up at me almost angrily. 'But he can't live... out of water... for long.' He takes another long shuddering breath. 'What if he's fallen out... of the door... in... into the desert?' Tears pour down onto his shirt.

'He won't have.' I'm *determined* he won't have.

'Or fallen down . . . in . . . into . . . the luggage compartment,' he stutters. 'Ohhhh . . . no!' He begins to sob again, so hard that words fail him.

'What, Tim?' I say. 'What is it?'

His words come in fits and starts. 'He'll . . . be climbing . . . all over . . . the bombs . . . down there.' My insides turn to wool. Could a terrapin set off a bomb? I feel sick. Should I tell the captain?

'Look, I'm sure he'll still be in the cabin, Tim. Really.'

David comes back. I look up at him questioningly. He shakes his head. Jamal moves around him to get to the back of the plane.

'Has anyone told the hijackers?' I ask.

'Don't think so,' David says.

'I think we should. They need to be careful where they're treading.'

David watches Jamal. 'Fred's probably not the most important thing in the world to them right now.'

Tim's voice rises. 'But he's important to me!'

'Of course he is, Tim.' I give David a look. 'Come on,' I say, desperate to go somewhere, do something else, to get Tim moving out of his grief. 'Let's go and tell Jamal. Then he can tell all the others.'

So we march down the plane. Jamal's standing guard with his gun slung over one shoulder. He's in the open space between the galley and the closed back door. Behind him are the four toilets. Even with the doors firmly closed, I can smell them from halfway down the cabin. As I approach, Jamal reaches for the water bottle on his belt, unscrews the cap and takes a swig – and that's when I see something moving by his foot.

It's Fred! I stop dead in my tracks, feel David on my shoulder. He's seen Fred too. 'Ah,' he says. 'Now what?'

'Why've you stopped?' Tim pushes under my arm.

Then, seeing Fred, he lurches forward, but David grabs him. 'Don't, Tim!' he hisses. 'You can't go rushing up to a guy with a gun.'

'Why? He's...' He looks up at David imploringly. 'He wouldn't hurt him –' he looks at me – 'would he? He wouldn't stamp...Anna! He wouldn't throw...like the guitar...' Tim swallows, can't continue.

'Just hang on, Tim,' I say. 'We need to make sure we do this right, get him back safely.' I look at David. 'I'll speak, OK? Don't say anything.'

I walk slowly towards Jamal.

'Hi,' I say, aware of the other two behind me watching Fred making a slow detour around Jamal's black boot.

'Hello,' Jamal replies calmly, but his expression is unsure.

'Jamal,' I say, 'Tim here's lost something.'

'Right...?' he says, looking enquiringly at Tim. 'What?'

'His terrapin.'

'Terrapin?' He frowns, not familiar with the word.

'A sort of little turtle that he keeps in a tin, in water.'

'Ah.' His brow clears.

'The thing is,' I say, 'we've been searching through the whole cabin for ages, and Tim's really upset at losing him and, well –' I pause and risk it – 'he's just by your foot.'

Jamal looks down.

I hold my breath. I hope desperately that he is kind, that I'm not wrong about him. *Don't be a cruel terrorist. Please. Not now.*

Jamal's face breaks into an amused smile. His body relaxes. He unslings his gun and leans it against the wall, kneels down and very gently scoops up Fred. We watch, rooted to the spot. Jamal looks up at us, delighted, then he nods, beckoning us to approach. He holds his hand out to Tim. Fred clambers onto Tim's hand, slowly as if tired of his adventure and wanting to go home.

'Thank you,' Tim whispers. 'Thank you *so* much.' He looks back at us, grinning. His eyes, still a little teary, are bright with happiness.

'I heard the English were crazy about pets,' Jamal smiles, 'but this one really *is* crazy.' He's relaxed and friendly. And I'm so relieved. 'How do you keep him in here?' Jamal asks, his eyes dancing with humour.

'In a tin!' Tim says. 'I'll show you!' He dashes off with Fred, calling happily back over his shoulder, 'He'll need to get back in the water anyway.'

Jamal smiles at David, and then at me, but it's obvious that Tim's going has left an awkward gap. I start to fill it. 'I hope you don't mind, Jamal, but I told Tim, and David here, your story.' I stop, feeling out of my depth. What *am* I doing? I plough on. 'You know, what you told me, about your parents. I hope you don't mind.'

'No, I don't mind,' Jamal says quietly, looking quizzically again at us. 'I hope it will help you to understand why we have to do this.' And I feel the strangeness of it all. English kids, hostages, unarmed, talking to a Palestinian, with live hand grenades on his belt, with bullets and a gun. But he's still human.

David isn't ready to forgive or understand though. 'So what did happen, after you lost your parents?' he asks.

Jamal shifts a little and a shadow passes over his strong features. 'My parents? After they were murdered?'

'Well, yes.'

'We walked with others that night –' his expression is faraway, thoughtful – 'with our neighbours, our friends, the teachers, the shopkeeper from the village – all fleeing their homes. We were the lucky ones. We were still alive. But we left with nothing, no food, just a little water.'

'I know the feeling,' David says drily, looking at me.

'Yes.' Jamal acknowledges it. 'But you will return to your homes. To your homeland.' He looks straight at us, his face open, his eyes clear. And I wonder if he knows something we don't, and feel a glimmer of hope.

He drops his head, shakes it, 'I'm sorry you are here, but we are desperate. We were destroyed then, completely dispossessed and driven out with nothing: no home, family, passport, possessions. No security, no education. Nothing.'

'And so, because of that, we may all be killed tomorrow,' David interrupts. 'I'm sorry about what happened to you, but why should I pay for it? And my family? And Anna's?'

'We just want the world to take some notice.' Jamal is insistent. 'We've tried everything. In the end, what else can we do? Tell me, what would you do?' He's challenging us, wanting us to understand.

'Look!' Tim appears, shattering the moment. He touches Jamal on the sleeve. 'This is Fred's tin!'

'Fred.' Jamal looks down at Tim. His face relaxes. His intensity disappears. 'You call him *Fred*?' He smiles. 'Like Fred Flintstone?' He continues looking in the tin. 'There is not much water in here for him.'

'It's evaporated in the heat,' I say.

'And, as you know,' David says with more than a hint of bitterness, 'there's hardly any water on board.'

'Here.' Jamal unhooks his water bottle from his belt. 'There's a little in here. Not much.' He tips it into Fred's tin. As the water glugs out, I lick my cracked lips and am aware of David swallowing uncomfortably. Would I drink Fred's water if I have to stay here much longer? Yes, I know now that I would.

'Thanks, Jamal,' Tim says. We all lean in, and watch Fred waggle his little webbed feet about and dip his head delightedly below the water.

'He'd got terribly dry wandering about,' Tim says. 'So, you see, *you've* saved his life *twice*.' He looks up at Jamal admiringly.

'Good.' Jamal smiles.

'Let's hope you can do that for us too then,' David says crisply. Jamal doesn't respond.

'Jamal,' says Tim, putting the tin on the floor and fixing the lid back on firmly, 'do you sleep in those trenches out there?'

'Yes.'

'And where did you learn to use your gun – and throw hand grenades?' Tim asks.

'Unfortunately we had to learn. It became obvious that the only way we will ever get the land back that we have lost is to fight for it.' He pauses, checks that we're all following. 'The world forgot about us for a very long time. Defending ourselves is part of our lives now.'

We're all silent for a moment. He continues, gesturing with his hands as he speaks. 'Imagine having to fight for the freedom to have a job, or to move from one place to another. Imagine—'

'Where did you live before this then?' Tim asks.

'In a refugee camp. Where else can you go, when you are driven from your land where you have lived all your life? I hope to go back to Palestine one day. All we want is to go back home, to our land. That is *all* that drives us.' He looks away at the porthole, his face in shadow.

'So after your parents died,' says David, 'who looked after you?'

'Relatives to begin with,' Jamal explains, 'but they were Palestinians, so they were driven off their land too. We all had to leave our country and come over the border to live in refugee camps here in Jordan, where we have been ever since.' He looks at each of us in turn. 'We are the people the world forgot.' He pauses, opens both palms. 'And this is what we have to do now, to get someone to hear us. We don't want to live in refugee camps for ever. Would you? Would you condemn *your* children to grow up homeless and angry as well?'

'We might not live to have children,' David swipes back under his breath.

'I'd be *really* mad if anyone did that to me,' Tim says.

Jamal nods. 'Some of us do go mad.'

'Yeah, Lady Mac for one,' says David.

'Who?' asks Jamal.

'The woman who comes on board every night,' I explain, 'to threaten us.'

'She's *really* scary,' Tim says.

'I knew she came to speak to you, but I didn't know she did that.' The three of us exchange glances. Jamal looks at us, hesitates, then seems to decide something. 'She thinks she's in charge here, but the real commander, the one who spoke to the reporters, is a good man. I cannot speak to her.'

'Why not?' asks David.

'She hates the English. They were the ones who gave our land away to the Jews, and she knows my mother was English.'

'You're half English?' says David, and I wonder what he feels about that.

'Yes, my mother came originally to Palestine to teach English. She fell in love with my father and never went back. My father brought her to the farm.' He looks down. 'At least they died together. They would have wanted it that way.' The light has gone from his eyes. They're hollow with the memory of it. 'Now I have them here, always, inside my heart.'

I'm moved by his words and desperately want him to know that we do understand something of his story. 'Jamal,' I say gently, 'we also know what it's like not to have a fixed home. All three of us – our parents are sent to different jobs all over the world every few years. You talk of land, but *we* don't have any. My parents don't have a home, an actual house or land that belongs to them, that they own. And when people ask me where I come from, I don't know what to say. I'm English, but I *come* from nowhere. There's nowhere in England I belong.'

'But England is your homeland.'

'Yes.'

'Can you go and live somewhere in England, your homeland, if you choose to?'

'Well, yes, I suppose so.'

'Well then, that is the difference. We are not allowed to go back to our homeland. They say it does not belong to us any more. We cannot go back there. Ever. *That* is why we are fighting. Fighting for our freedom to return.'

I feel David's restlessness. 'I heard that you were looking for Jews on this plane,' he says, 'but there weren't any; that you really wanted to hijack an El Al plane.'

'Yes,' Jamal says.

'Why El Al?' asks Tim.

'It's a Jewish airline. It's the Jews who have taken our land.'

'But a long time ago,' David counters, 'weren't *they* forced to leave their homes in Palestine that they'd lived in for hundreds of years? They'd have felt persecuted then, that they had no land, no homeland of *their* own.'

Tim shakes his head. 'This is *very* confusing.'

David turns to him. 'Yes, it is. And more recently, millions of Jews were killed in the Holocaust during the Second World War. So after the war thousands of Jews from all over the world went to live in Palestine, wanting to be safe.'

'But it was really *our* land,' Jamal insists.

David considers his point. 'Yes, but the argument about who that land belongs to goes back hundreds of years.' He turns back to Tim. 'The Jews and the Arab Palestinians each believe it is *their* homeland and after the Second World War it led to terrible fights. And it hasn't got any better since then. And now we're caught up in it.'

'What a mess,' says Tim.

'I know. How do you sort that one out?' David agrees.

'By hating each other?' I ask. They all look at me.

Tim sighs. 'I don't know *why* the grown-ups don't sort it out properly. What's wrong with them all?'

The Giant comes down the aisle, catches Jamal's eye and tilts his head towards the front.

'I have to go,' Jamal says. 'It's been good talking to you. I'll see you later on, maybe this afternoon.'

'Jamal,' I say quickly, 'you said you thought we'd get to go back home. What about the deadline?'

'I believe you'll be OK,' he replies. 'There's still time. We still have a little time.' The Giant calls him again. 'I have to go.'

Everything is unresolved. *Everything.*

We follow him down the aisle and watch as he crouches in the doorway, calls to someone below and hands down his gun. The sun catches his hair as he starts to descend the ladder and then he's gone.

David's looking at me. '*You* seem to like him.'

'Don't you?'

He shrugs. 'Not sure.'

'Really?'

'He's prepared to kill us, Anna. Blow us all up if he has to. How can he possibly justify that? There's nothing I've heard him say that makes *that* all right.'

Tim leans forward in his seat. 'Well, I think he's nice. And I like him even more since he gave Fred his water.'

I sit down in one of my seats across from the boys and stare out of the window at the clumps of rock casting their shadows across the sand. I think of the restless wind chiselling away at the stone, making more sand, endless miles of it. And I think of the black cloud of the deadline creeping ever closer.

Noon on Saturday, she said. Tomorrow. So why did Jamal say we had *time*? That seems like no time at all to me.

And the words arrive from nowhere. *The sands of time are running out.* They make me think of the egg timer on the kitchen dresser: two glass bulbs, one above the other, in a wooden frame. Turn it upside down, and the pink sand in the top runs into the bottom in a thin straight line. Fine sand falling through space.

Until time runs out and the glass is empty.

39

16.00 hrs

Rosemary and Celia deliver each of us a small cup of water. I sip it very slowly; feel the silveryness of it slide across my dry tongue and down my blotting paper throat. I imagine it rolling lightly like mercury into my stomach. All too soon my little cup is empty, but at least the water softens my headache for a while.

And the afternoon slips by. No news comes. No one seems to be *doing* anything, well except the deadline, rushing towards us like a runaway train. I feel increasingly restless. I pace up and down the plane, past Rosemary fussing over the baby grizzling on his mother's knee, past the Newtons arguing about who forgot to bring spare batteries for the radio, past Maria, still looking fragile, past Celia, smoking with Alan, her hair wonderfully dishevelled.

Everyone seems to be smoking. The air is thick with it. The ashtrays are overflowing. Everywhere stinks of stale smoke, the upholstery, our clothes, our hair. I've even seen the twins taking a surreptitious puff.

As I walk past Jim, he offers me a cigarette. 'Well,' he grins, 'if you can't beat 'em, join 'em.' And so I do. What the hell? Nothing matters any more.

I draw the smoke in. And I can't explain how incredibly satisfying it is right now to do something that's bad for you, that tastes so revolting, something *different*, something self-inflicted.

'Keeps the old appetite at bay too, as well as the nerves,' Jim says. When he smiles I notice that his eyes disappear completely.

'Thanks,' I say. And then my stomach rumbles. It sounds cavernous. 'Oh, dear, sorry.' *How embarrassing*. I smile apologetically. 'Bit hungry.'

'Och, we're all rumbling like underground trains,' he says kindly.

I change the subject. 'I've been wondering,' I say. 'You know I helped Rosemary collect the untouched food and drinks on the first day, well, there was more stuff in there that was only half eaten. So why, since we're all so desperately hungry, don't we eat it now?'

'Ah! If only,' he says. 'But imagine what it looks like, in this heat, two days later? I wouldn't like to open those trolleys up again. The smell will be terrible and it'll all be covered in mould and full of bacteria. Shame, eh?'

'Big shame. We should have eaten it then.'

'We should indeed.'

I stub my cigarette out in the overflowing ashtray, thank him again and drift back to my seat. My mouth feels disgusting, but it did anyway, and, like Jim says, it's taken the edge off my hunger for a moment.

I sit disconsolately doing nothing for a while, then see Jamal coming down the aisle on his way to the back for his next shift.

He stops by my seat. 'Hi.' He looks hopeful, then unsure. 'You all right?'

I shrug, look away, lean against the window. I want him to see how fed up I am, that it's all his fault.

He hesitates, then, refusing to be affected by my behaviour, perches on the end armrest. 'So are you going crazy yet?' He smiles.

'Yes, I am,' I say. 'And it's not funny.'

But weirdly, it's then that I understand what he was talking about earlier. And it occurs to me for the first time that he is risking his life by being here, that even if we're freed, he may very well be killed. Maybe he's feeling as scared as I am.

I turn to him, feeling more like conversing. 'What did you think, when my buckle caught on your belt?'

He raises dark eyebrows and says, mock severe, 'I thought you were serious trouble.' Then his face turns solemn. 'But I saw how you dealt with fear,' he says. 'I know you are strong.'

I shake my head. 'You don't know me at all, Jamal. But what about you? Are you strong?'

'Yes. And I have a good heart like yours.'

'Do you?' I look disbelieving.

'You see only the gun,' he says. 'The hand grenades... When you are dispossessed of everything else, your body is all you have left to fight with.' He looks at me. 'But of course you cannot see who I really am. How can you?'

'Well... it's not *that* easy.'

'It's impossible to see properly in this place,' he mutters, as if talking to himself. And it's true. Everything's a muddle in here. Out of control. I think of Maria, about what happened to her.

'Jamal, where's the other guy, the thin one with black hair?'

'Oh.' He looks down, embarrassed.

'We haven't seen him today,' I insist.

'No.'

'No one's talking to us about it, but something happened last night with him and one of the girls from first class.'

'Yes.'

'She was incredibly upset.'

'Yes.'

I wait. He looks away, then back at me. 'He's not allowed on the plane any more,' he says.

'Well, yes, I noticed,' I say impatiently. 'So what happened?'

He pauses, then takes a breath. 'He touched her.' I feel the shock of the words, the idea of it.

'He touched and frightened her,' he adds, and I'm quietened.

'He's been disciplined,' he continues. But I don't want to know any more.

'My friend, the tall guy,' he carries on, 'he's spoken to your captain – and to the girl.' He shakes his head angrily. 'He was so stupid.'

Suddenly I feel a wave of exhaustion. I stare at Jamal's arm lying along the top of the seats, at his khaki shirt cuff, the gold face and black strap of his watch. *This day might be my last. His last.*

My throat constricts, tears rise. I mustn't blink or they'll fall and he'll see. I really want to ask him something though, but no words come for a moment.

Jamal waits, watching my face.

I take a deep breath.

'If we *are* released tomorrow, what will happen to you? I mean . . . afterwards?' I ask. 'Aren't you scared?'

'Yes, I am. Of course I am. But some of us aren't.'

'Like who?'

'My tall friend.'

'We call him the Giant.'

He smiles. 'He is, a giant among men. I've known him since I was little. His light went out long before he came here.'

'What do you mean?'

'I mean that he doesn't fear death. He has lost too much already: his wife, his girls, his son. He says he doesn't want to stay any more. He says dying for the cause is all he can do now, so that others might one day go home.' He leans forward and looks at me. 'Can you understand that?'

'Yes, I think so.' I'm aware of the rise and fall of his chest.

'Is it the first time you've had to face death?' he asks.

I nod.

'Don't be too afraid. In the end it will make you stronger.'

Easy enough to say, I think, but I let it go.

'What will you do,' I ask, 'when this is over? If . . .'

'If I survive?'

'Yes.'

'Until I can return to my homeland, my dream is to go to university, maybe in Beirut, in the Lebanon. I have sent my brother to our aunt there. She writes often, begging me to come too.'

'Well, then you must. How can you *not* get away from all this?' But of course, it isn't a case of just jumping on a bus. 'You should go,' I say. 'I know someone at school who lives there . . .' I stop, realising that what I'm saying is going nowhere.

'Are you on your way back to school in England?' he asks.

'Yes.'

'Then you are lucky. You can learn about the world, and afterwards go out into it.'

'So can you.'

He shrugs. 'Maybe, one day.' He looks away, then back. 'Your parents are in Bahrain?'

'I don't know. They were due to fly home today. If we're released, I hope they'll be waiting for me.'

He frowns. 'They will never abandon you, Anna.'

'No.' Suddenly I feel the weight of his words. As I try to control my emotions, he waits quietly, looking down the aisle, his black boot resting against the chair fabric.

'Come, Anna, no more sad thoughts,' he says eventually. 'Instead I must thank you for letting me practise my English. I love to hear it, it reminds me always of my mother.'

When he goes, I feel calmer for having spoken to him, as though a little of my fear has been smoothed and folded away, as though, just for a while, I've been somewhere else.

Through my little window, I watch the sun sink and the desert burn gold and, as the sand loses its heat, sheets of gossamer-thin clouds unfurl high up.

And night falls on our third day.

40

20.00 hrs

It's our last night, the last night before the deadline tomorrow. What can anyone say? What can anyone do? We can only carry on. I'm stuck in a cycle of sudden and awful remembering, followed by anxiety, fear, exhaustion and forgetting.

I wish I could stop thinking, unhook myself from my mind.

Instead David, Tim and I play Scrabble. We sip our water ration and eat another scrap of unleavened bread. David is intensely irritated by everything: by the Giant pacing up and down, by dropping his Scrabble tiles, by the annoying jiggle of the hurricane lamps. In the end, we're all irritated by each other. Like the bundles of dynamite, our fuses are short.

I try pretending nothing significant is happening. I push dangerous thoughts to one side, and when I fail, I have to stand up, leave the others, walk away, recover, return, sit back down again.

In the middle of all this, Mrs Green finds two batteries in the bottom of her washbag that fit the Newtons' radio.

Everyone crowds round in good time for Big Ben. The radio buzzes, crackles into life. The newscaster's voice is crisp:

'*The Palestinian guerrilla spokesman said tonight that unless there is a last-minute reprieve and the British government frees Leila Khaled, the guerrilla held in London, the airliner and the hostages will be blown up tomorrow morning.*'

There's an awful silence. I feel like I'm drowning.

The mother of the baby turns away and starts to cry. Mrs Green takes her daughter in her arms and hugs her. The little girl moans and wriggles free. Mr Newton snaps the radio off. 'Bloody government,' he cries. He's beside himself. 'Christ! What are they thinking? No doubt those bloody bastards are sitting in Downing Street sipping a nice glass of port before bed. Don't worry about us!' He slams his hand down on the seat in front. 'We'll just sit here in this metal bloody time bomb, trussed up with explosives.' His face is purple with rage.

The captain puts a hand on his shoulder, 'Now, Tom, that's no way to speak.' Mr Newton shrugs him off, but the captain keeps going. 'I'm sure there's a great deal of activity going on behind the scenes,' he says to the rest of us. 'That's what we have to believe. It's an incredibly tense time, but we all really must stay calm and weather it.'

Mr Newton attempts to stand up. 'Well, let's see what our captors have to say, shall we? Let's talk to *them*, shall we?'

The captain bars his way. 'I don't think that's a good idea, Tom. No point causing trouble at this stage. And no point upsetting everyone else.'

Jim steps up. 'Come along now, everybody.' He puts his arms out and starts herding people away from the Newtons' seats. 'Let's not get carried away. No point in panicking.'

Rosemary joins him, and guides the blonde sisters back up the aisle. 'We need to stay calm,' she says to them, 'and try to get some sleep.' She puts a hand out as she passes by and touches me on the shoulder. 'OK?'

I nod, but I'm beyond misery, my last hope has been shattered. A deep dread settles in my stomach. Another day of negotiations has ended with no release for us.

David collapses into the seat opposite, looking like he's been punched in the stomach. He glances across at me, his face drawn. 'The only thing that can save us now is a miracle.' He wipes his forehead and his face with his hands. 'Unless you think that good-luck badge of yours can do it.'

I turn hopelessly away.

The dynamite charges are in place. We're locked in. Eventually the hurricane lamps are turned low and the night feels suddenly longer, colder and more hostile than ever.

I try to sleep but, like everyone else, I just lie waiting for morning.

I think about Marni, how she's not afraid to ignore silly rules. I see her hair, her scarf, the man's wristwatch halfway up her arm. I remember how Dad's jokes misfire, how he dries my hair with a towel, how once he taught us army hand signals on a deserted beach. And I think of the boys. Oh, the boys – I love them all so much that it hurts. And I think how lucky I've been to know them, to spend my short life with them.

The void around me grows and expands, and my tears pour out into the dark.

Eventually I sleep fitfully, restlessly. At intervals throughout the night my eyes jerk open, my heart races, thumping in my ears. And for a split second I don't know where I am, what I'm so terrified of.

Then I sit upright – and remember.

I pull up the blind, stare out of the window. When we were small and upset, Marni would take us to look out at the night, at the moon and the stars. And there is the moon's sheen, and there are the stars, calm and bright in the black firmament. But where's Marni? I need her so much.

41

Saturday 12th September 1970

06.00 hrs

When I wake again, it's that soft time after dawn. Threads of pink clouds lie in lines above the horizon. In the trenches around the plane, old campfires glow red-grey. A long line of camels treads rhythmically on a distant ridge, each step throwing up a puff of sand.

At the front of the plane, Alan has his arm around Rosemary. Is he comforting her? Has something happened? Across the aisle from them, the captain talks earnestly to Jim. Have they heard something?

I watch the Giant pass a piece of paper to the captain, who sits on the arm of a nearby seat to read it. Have they released Leila Khaled? Is it good news? Are we going home? I can't see the captain's expression. He turns to Jim, says something. Jim nods and beckons to the other crew members. They move to huddle around the captain. What are they deciding? Who is going to be shot first? My stomach lurches. I feel so sick. I never really believed this moment would come. But it has.

It really has.

I lean across the aisle. 'Something's happening.'

David and Tim crouch up on their seats to look.

'The captain's giving instructions to the crew,' David says.

'What for?' asks Tim.

'Dread to think.'

I feel light-headed and sit down. I open my table and press my forehead onto it. My whole body is in a revolt of fear. I can feel the nausea rising.

'D'you mean . . . ?' Tim says slowly.

The captain stands up. The crew take their seats.

'Good morning, everyone,' the captain says. 'A moment, please. A moment of your time. I have something important to tell you.'

Saliva rushes into my mouth. I am going to be sick. I scrabble to find the bag in the seat pocket.

'Would those people still standing sit down, please?'

There's a great shuffling about; the bald man in front is trying to put something in his overhead locker. We wait while he carefully folds his coat. I want to scream at him to stop, to sit down! Eventually he does.

There's an uncanny stillness. I open the sick bag and turn away towards the window.

'It's good news.' The captain smiles. 'We're going home!'

His words are greeted with a great uproar of clapping and whooping. I slump back in my seat, dropping the sick bag. I look over at the boys, stunned. Tim is jumping up and down with his arms in the air. He leaps on David, hugging him. Then he scrambles over, picks up my limp hand, turns it over and, grinning, quickly kisses the palm. Then he's off to see the twins.

At the front, Celia is hugging Alan, the bald man shakes the captain's hand, the blonde girls sob, their arms around each other. Rosemary hugs Sarah and plants a big kiss on the baby's forehead. Behind me, Mr Newton is slapping everyone he can reach on the back. I look over at David. His smile is a mile wide. He comes over and gives me a long hug.

'How about that?' he says.

I stare at him, speechless, a great sob gripping me. He puts his arms back around me again. 'We're going to be OK, Anna. We're going to be OK.' I nod into his chest and I don't want to pull away.

When the clamour finally dies down, the captain, smiling broadly, continues. 'I expect you'd like to know the details. The British government has negotiated with the Palestinians. We don't know everything yet, but I have a letter here from the chief British negotiator, which I believe to be genuine, otherwise I wouldn't raise your hopes. He says that the plan is for us to leave the plane at about two p.m. today. Minibuses will apparently be sent from Amman to take us back into the city, where we'll be put up overnight, some in hotels, others – mainly the unaccompanied young people – will stay with diplomatic families in their homes. Initially the guerrillas refused to accept the decision made by their main commando leadership, the central committee, but in the end an agreement of sorts was reached. We are to be released on humanitarian grounds. The King of Jordan has arranged for a Jordanian Airlines plane to fly us to Cyprus tomorrow morning, where we'll transfer to an RAF flight home. That's all I know at this point.' Relief is written all over his exhausted face. He pauses and looks around the cabin. 'I don't have to tell you that the situation is still grave and potentially very volatile. There is much that can happen before we are on our way. We must be calm and polite and not create any tension *at all* between now and two o'clock this afternoon; nothing that will put the plan at risk. I'm sure I can count on your co-operation. When I give the command, we'll need to proceed to the waiting buses quietly. If we behave as we have done so far, we may all leave in one piece. I'll talk to you all again at one forty-five. In the meantime, please speak to a member of the crew if you have any questions, but remember none of us have any information about the plan other than what I have just told you. Again, I urge you to remain calm and quiet. No rocking the boat at this critical phase, please.'

Everything is different. The relief inside the plane seems to change the air we breathe. If I didn't know it to be impossible, I'd think the air con was back on.

But then, as the minutes pass, we become more muted. Because now we have hope, and with that comes a new fear – the fear of what we might lose. We're so close to actual freedom, but now anything, anything at all, could go wrong.

I don't seem able to calm the turmoil in my exhausted mind. I feel strung out, balancing between relief, elation and a quiet dread, the dread that someone or something might jeopardise this fragile chance of freedom. What if someone on one of the other planes...?

But I mustn't think about that. There's no point. What matters now is getting *off* this plane, getting as far away as possible from the huge bomb we're sitting in.

I pack my things into my bag very slowly: *Wuthering Heights*, the almost empty pot of Nivea, my BOAC fan, my badge, Marni's letter... and as I do, my anxiety and confusion grow.

I'm going to live. I want to leave. And yet. And yet leaving the plane, going outside, away from it, feels incredibly dangerous too. We have no idea what's out there, what we're getting into next.

42

London - 09.00 hrs
(British Summer Time)

Marni looks down at the plate of food her sister has cooked for her breakfast, at the lacy egg white and the yellow globe of yolk, and her eyes glaze over.

'Come on, Marni,' Diana says gently. 'It might be a long day.'

'I know...but...'

Her sister puts an arm around her and kisses her on the forehead. 'You must eat.'

'Yes, it's just...I don't know what to say to them any more,' she says hopelessly. The sound of the television filters in from the sitting room, where the two boys are watching.

Suddenly Mark shouts out. Marni starts to her feet, but Diana puts a hand on her shoulder. 'I'll go,' she says, and marches out of the room. 'Now, you two little tinkers, what's going on?'

The egg on Marni's plate congeals. The bacon has rigor mortis. They've been given a phone number to call. She's tried it twice already, but hasn't been able to get through. James was so frustrated that he borrowed Di's car this morning and has driven in to the Foreign Office, saying he'll call if he finds out anything new. Marni listens. Was that the phone?

'Marni!' The shout comes from the sitting room. 'Quick!'

She leaps to her feet and dashes to the open doorway.

The news is on.

'They're letting them go!'

Oh my God. They're letting them go.

Marni puts a hand to her temple and slumps against the door frame.

Sam stares at her. 'Mum?' He gets up and runs over, puts his arms around her. 'Mum?'

She wraps him up and squeezes him tight. 'It's OK,' she murmurs. 'It's OK, my darling. I'm just happy.' She wipes her eyes quickly with the back of her hand, then smiles down into his eyes. 'See?'

He looks hard at her. 'Your mouth is,' he says, 'but your eyes aren't yet.'

'Will Anna be OK now, Mum?' Mark says from the floor.

'Yes,' Marni says. 'She'll be absolutely fine.'

43

Revolutionary Airstrip, Jordan - 14.30 hrs

Six dirty white, bullet-scarred minibuses draw up alongside the plane, and everyone is ordered to leave the aircraft. I look at my place, my row of three chairs, my little window, my overhead locker and the fold-down trays. I look at the floor where I've slept. This has been my place, where I've *been*, where I've lived through all this. Where I've hidden, slept, dreamed, laughed, cried.

It pulls me back.

Suddenly I don't want to leave it. If I do, it will be for ever.

In a blur, I pick up my bag, file down the aisle, and, as I wait in the queue to be helped down the ladder, I look at the line of subdued passengers standing quietly below in the burning sun. They look scruffy, disordered, rumpled. Older. There's little conversation. Even the baby is silent. Hands are tightly held: the Newtons, the blonde sisters, Mrs Green stoops to tie Susan's shoelace.

As soon as I am down too, I look around the aircraft for

Jamal and the Giant. There's been no sign of them since the captain's announcement. I'd really like to say goodbye. Instead I see the neat dark figure of Lady Mac watching from the shadow of the tail. Is that the man with the bomb standing next to her? I turn away to join the queue waiting to collect luggage from under the other wing.

Rosemary is in front. She turns and smiles at me. 'Isn't this great...?' She stops. 'Is everything all right?

'Yes, of course.' I give her a wan smile. 'Just feel a bit odd.'

She looks relieved. 'I know what you mean. We'll all feel a bit odd over the next few weeks. It's going to take time to get back to normal. But imagine, Anna – a shower! Sleeping in a real bed! Seeing your family.' She turns back to collect her luggage. And of course I know she's right.

I can see the two other planes properly now. Their passengers are milling about under them, collecting their luggage, and there are minibuses parked there too, waiting to take them into Amman.

Tim and David have already collected their cases and have gone on ahead to queue by our minibuses. It takes ages to locate my case, and, by the time I do find it, I glimpse Tim climbing into the minibus behind the lead Jeep, which has a large Palestinian flag fluttering from its radio aerial. The minibuses from the other two planes have set off and are already wending their way across the desert, leaving a long trail of dust behind them. I think of the people in them, who were held even longer than us. What must they be feeling like now?

I'm told to board the last minibus in the line and feel a great wave of disappointment at being separated from David and Tim. I climb in and sit in the single seat by the window behind the driver and the guard. The door slams shut and we move off, flanked by Jeeps with guerrillas I don't recognise. Our driver, wearing his black beret at a jaunty angle, swings the wheel left, then right, struggling to avoid the deep fissures in the hard sand. The guard sitting next to him in the front cradles his rifle on his lap, his headdress obscuring his face.

I stare back at the three planes. They look smaller already, and incredibly isolated in the middle of the empty desert. And, although I'm relieved to be going home, I suddenly feel worried about what will happen to them? Will they fly home one day too?

I lived in that plane for four days, felt safe in it, as well as in terrible danger. And now I don't feel safe at all. I don't really know where I'm going, or even if I'll get there alive. I'm just shut in again, but this time with only a dozen people, who I still hardly know. No Rosemary, no Jim, no captain, not even the Newtons or Susan and Mrs Green. Not even the baby. Just Maria slumped at the back next to the bald man, both smoking.

The three planes are small as Dinky Toys now. And when we drive down a slope into a wadi, a dry river channel, they vanish from view – and I feel bereft.

The temperature rises inside the van, so I slide my window open to let some air in, but it's blisteringly hot outside too. I'm desperately thirsty. Our last water ration was hours ago. I run my finger round the tin of Nivea and rub the very last smear of cream into my dry lips.

While we lurch and bounce over the dry earth and water-smoothed stones that form the bed of the wadi, I imagine the river as it once was, millions of years ago with giraffe, zebra, hippos and elephants grazing. Suddenly, I see two black tanks hunched ahead on the horizon and feel a shunt of adrenaline. Are they friendly? Will they fire at us? Am I going to die now, here, after all?

There's muttering among the passengers, and then everyone falls quiet. As we get closer, I see the huge tyre tracks and the gun turret, and figures leaning against the great creature's flanks. Closer still, and I see they're drinking from metal cups and smoking. As we pass by, turning left through a gap in a barbed-wire fence onto a rough murram road, the soldiers raise their cups as if toasting us.

Every so often, in between long stretches of road, we have to stop at PFLP roadblocks. The driver shows his papers and sometimes exchanges news and information. The PFLP seems to control this side of Amman, and the road is littered with burning tyres and rocks, debris from barricades and from fighting. I can hear bursts of gunfire, faintly to begin with, then worryingly close. We pass several low buildings that have been reduced to rubble. Further off I see a twisted plume of thick black smoke rising into the air. And I begin to wonder if we'll ever make it into the centre of Amman, or escape home before the country explodes into civil war. And if it does, then what? What will happen to us?

At the next roadblock a line of brown-and-gold camels walk past with their heads outstretched, ignoring the revving Jeeps, the minibuses and the intermittent gunfire, just treading the desert as they always have done.

When the road becomes tarmac, we travel faster between the roadblocks. I sit back, close my eyes and welcome the warm wind on my face. It ripples through my hair, cools my neck. The rhythm begins to lull me and I doze. But soon I sense the minibus slowing down again and open my eyes to see that we've reached the outskirts of the city. Crowds of people are going about their business. There are bike bells and car horns and stifling exhaust fumes. When I smell food cooking, my stomach clenches. I salivate and am consumed by hot, sick waves of hunger. I look longingly at the bunches of bananas hanging from stalls, the crates of oranges, the mounds of carrots. A woman on a veranda drinks mint tea from a glass.

We pass a butcher's shop, a man unloading sacks of flour from a truck, a boy selling cold water from an ice chest fixed to the front of his bicycle. *Moya barrida*, he shouts, waving at me. Cold water. *Moya barrida*. Can't we stop and buy some? But perhaps we're nearly there.

I'll drink water soon enough, I tell myself. As much as I want.

We're stationary in a busy road approaching the InterContinental Hotel. And suddenly I'm aware that there's no sign of the PFLP Jeeps that accompanied us. Somewhere along the road, they must have quietly melted away. Up ahead I can see a huge crowd of people. When they spot our minibuses, they start running towards us, dodging through the traffic. Reporters with cameras on their shoulders trailing loops of wire, some with notebooks, some carrying reels of film, others with earphones, boom microphones. And my heart sinks. I don't want to fight my way through them, to have to be filmed and answer questions. I just want to get inside the hotel and find David and Tim again.

44

Amman, Jordan - 16.30 hrs

One of the reporters outside the InterContinental Hotel runs up to our minibus window and jogs alongside. 'How did they treat you?' he shouts, his yellow tie flying over one shoulder. But the minibus lurches forward, accelerates away and the man disappears behind us.

When we slow down in the traffic, he catches up again. 'Were they violent?' he shouts, his brown hair flopping. There's sweat on his top lip. 'Did they torture you? Was anyone abused?' There's a shocked silence inside the minibus before it edges forward again.

Suddenly a huge, grey boom microphone is thrust in through my window, forcing my head against the back of my seat, pushing into my face. As the man keeps pace, it jiggles up and down. The stale smell of it is sickening.

'Say something! Say something!' the man shouts at me.

His colleague comes alongside, his TV camera whirring.

Fury stirs in my blood: 'LEAVE US ALONE!' I yell.

The stinking microphone retreats. I slam my window shut and lock it. There's nervous laughter and a smattering of applause from behind. Someone pats me on the back. But all I can feel are my eyes filling, hot tears falling, pouring down.

The driver parks outside the hotel, drags on the handbrake and comes round to open the side door. I pull off the scarf tying back my hair and use it to wipe my face dry.

Then I step out into the scrum.

Picking up my case, I try to run the gauntlet through the shouting, jostling crowd of reporters waiting on the steps of the hotel. The noise is overwhelming and I hardly have the strength to batter my way through. Eventually someone grabs my arm and pulls me out of the crowd. The doors swing shut behind me and I'm inside, standing in the foyer in a mêlée of passengers, crew and uniformed staff, who are herding everyone around to the right. I can't see David and Tim anywhere, just our aircrew being siphoned off to the left.

Behind me there's a shout as a bunch of reporters surge past the hotel doormen. The reception and security staff dash to head them off. There are scuffles and swearing. Eventually the front doors are slammed closed and locked; the reporters outside bang continuously on the glass.

I glimpse several men in a doorway wearing suits and holding clipboards. As I pass one he asks my name and ticks me off his list. I'm ushered into a large air-conditioned room, the walls hung with old oil paintings in ornate gold frames. There is a large arrangement of flowers in a vase on the table, big curved white lilies with pointed leaves looking calm and dignified.

I search for David and Tim, determined to find them. I try

to squeeze through the crowd in front, but my case is too bulky, so I drop it. I can pick it up later. But then a burly official in navy uniform, still panting slightly from his exertions with the reporters, motions for me to stay put. He stands so close that I'm enveloped in his musky aftershave.

There are so many people in the room, all looking dishevelled, crumpled, traumatised. Babies cry, white-faced women clutch at each other in relief, couples huddle together for comfort. The air is electric with anxiety.

Two American women stand in front of me, swapping stories.

'Well, right at the very beginning,' says one of them, 'I saw her scrabbling in her purse and holding out a wad of dollars to this young hijacker, like he was a highwayman or something. He just looked at her, really dignified, and said. "We are not robbers, madam. We are fighting for our freedom."'

'No!' The other woman looks at her, thrilled.

They're interrupted by a man standing on the raised dais at the far end of the long room. He's wearing a slick-looking grey suit and tie and keeps clearing his throat. Though I strain to hear, I can only make out the occasional word. Who is he? The ambassador? A diplomat?

And then I think, What does it matter?

I'm so weary and empty that I slump down on the floor and lean against the back wall of the room. The official looks down at me in surprise. I stare pointedly away. I'm tired of being told what to do.

Up on the wall to my left is a clock with gilt ornaments around its wide, cracked enamel face. Its two black hands point to four thirty-five. I take off my watch, set the time and wind it again.

Staring into the crowd of legs in front of me, I recognise Mrs Newton's flat brown sandals, the backs of Maria's knees and Susan's cloth doll hanging down, looking dejected. There's a flash of maroon blazer, but no sign of Tim's lace-ups, or David's flip-flops. Mr Newton breaks free from the crowd, blows his nose loudly and examines the contents.

I look away in disgust and spot Sarah and her baby standing almost directly in front of me. Sarah kisses him on the cheek and jiggles him up and down. His little bare legs dangle and kick, and I have a sudden urge to hold one of those fat little feet, with their perfect tiny nails.

The noise in the room drops a notch as a woman's voice filters in overhead. It is higher-pitched and seems a bit easier to make out.

'... group of diplomats' wives,' she says. '... kindly offering to look after ... children ... take home ... meal, bath, sleep ... tomorrow's flight ... door marked A ...'

Sarah turns and spots me. 'I don't suppose you'd hold him for a moment,' she says, 'while I get something warmer for him to wear? This air conditioning's freezing, isn't it?'

She passes the baby into my arms. I feel the soft suede of his head brush my chin and breathe in his milky smell. He feels so solidly alive, a warm bundle of flesh. He turns his head and looks at me with eyes full of wonder.

'Hello,' I say, smiling down. 'Hello, you,' and I jiggle him a little, like Sarah does. He gurgles and wobbles about, and I hold him more tightly. Then he reaches out a chubby little hand and grabs my hair.

The crowd in front has started to thin now, and I just glimpse Tim and David being hustled through a door at the end of the room. Tim turns to look back, his eyes searching. I try to wave, to stop him, but I can't. I'd drop the baby.

I'm last to be called forward, the last to go through Door A for unaccompanied children. I burst through, excited to catch up with David and Tim at last – and am devastated to find that they're not there in the room beyond.

45

17.00 hrs

The only person in the room is a tall woman with thin brown hair pulled back in a small bun. She has a long, English face and wears an old-fashioned cotton dress belted at the waist. Her flat open-toed shoes are just like Granny's – navy leather with twists at the front.

'Hello, my dear, you must be Anna.' Her brown eyes are kind behind pale blue-rimmed glasses. 'I'm Mrs Hamilton.' I take the hand offered and shake it. Her grip is surprisingly strong.

'Now –' she licks her thin lips quickly – 'I've not had children of my own,' she says, making nervous, bird-like movements, 'but I do volunteer at the local orphanage, so you're not such a strange species to me after all.' She laughs. It's an awkward dry sound that feels like it needs practice. 'They said sweets, but I thought fruit.' She offers me a small Tupperware box.

'Thank you!' I say. I lift the lid and feast my eyes on the jewel-coloured fruit: two fat glistening dates, two moons of mango, a chunk of pineapple and two thick slices of peeled orange.

'Go on, dear,' Mrs Hamilton says. But I need no encouragement and polish it all off very quickly. Nothing has ever tasted so wonderful. When I start licking the juice off my filthy fingers, she offers me a napkin. Then she leads the way down several long sage-green corridors to a sleek black car parked round the back of the hotel. We stow my suitcase in the boot and climb in.

Mrs Hamilton drives away through the shaded, winding back streets. 'It's a bit of a maze, I'm afraid,' she says, as we pass a row of air-conditioning units dripping rusty water down scarred walls. 'But we'll avoid the press this way.'

We swing down wider roads and skirt roundabouts, before joining the heavy traffic in the city centre. Battered overloaded buses spew exhaust fumes into the car. Bikes and taxis press alongside. Through gaps between buildings, I glimpse telegraph line looping across stretches of wasteland and dead grass pricking up through hot sand. And there is the sun burning a hole on the horizon.

The road opens out a little and I can see that we're surrounded by hills covered in small white houses. As she drives, Mrs Hamilton points out tourist attractions, but I can't concentrate. When we climbed into the car, she handed me a bottle of water, apologising for not giving it to me first, and it's sitting on my lap.

I can't stop looking at it.

I wait for a break in the chatter to ask, 'Can I drink my water now, please, Mrs Hamilton?'

'Oh, my dear, of course you can. You're bound to be a bit thirsty.'

I unscrew the lid. A whole bottle to myself! This is what being all right is, having a stomach full of fruit *and* enough water to drink. I take a tiny sip, feel the cold wetness running down into the dry heat of my throat. I drink a little more. The cold winds its way down into my stomach. I put the lid back on, automatically rationing the rest.

The spicy smell of the souk wafts in through my open window. I imagine the cool, narrow criss-crossing passages crowded with people, squawking chickens, tables weighed down with bales of cloth, vegetables, coffee and spices.

We turn left down a road with dual-ridged tracks and lined with date palms. A group of camels sit folded like cats on the bare earth. A moth-eaten donkey, weighed down with firewood, stands tied to a tree, and there's a scattering of goats eating cardboard from a rubbish pile.

'Where are all the other young people going to stay, Mrs Hamilton?'

'Oh, at various diplomatic family houses. We were asked to offer hospitality and, I'm afraid, I said I could only take the one. Will you be all right on your own?'

'I expect so,' I reply, feeling a sense of dread at the thought.

When we arrive at Mrs Hamilton's house, the turbaned guard at the gate salutes and lifts the barrier. We go down a gravel drive into a wide, white-walled garden and park in front of marble steps leading up to an imposing black front door with a brass knocker. A white-liveried servant opens it, and stands back for us to pass.

'Anna will be in the Blue Room, Hassan,' she says. 'She'll need a bath and then a tray of supper in the kitchen at about seven.'

'Yes, madam.'

I follow her through into a large sitting room with sofas and a grand piano under an enormous gilt mirror. Tall French windows open onto the garden. Mrs Hamilton sits down in a plush red armchair and points to the chintz sofa. Birdsong breezes in through the French windows. It feels unreal, like I've been dropped into a Bond movie.

'I hope you won't mind having a tray in the kitchen,' Mrs Hamilton says. 'It's just we have people for dinner tonight.'

'No, not at all,' I reply.

'I imagine you'd value a little peace anyway, in the circumstances.' She blinks behind her glasses and then smiles a tense little smile. 'You young people are very resilient, so I'm told. Do you feel resilient, Anna?'

'Well ... I ...'

Mrs Hamilton senses she's been clumsy and changes the subject. 'We've had Hassan for ten years now.' She takes off her glasses and wipes them with a white lace hanky she keeps under her bra strap. 'He's a Palestinian, you know, and like a member of the family. If there's anything you need, just call him. There's a bell in your room.'

'Thank you.' And I wonder whether Hassan knows the Giant or Jamal – or any of the others.

'That's all right, dear. It's the least we can do after your ordeal. I expect you'd like an early night? Your plane to Cyprus, where you'll pick up the flight to London, leaves at six tomorrow morning. We'll have to get you to the airport pretty early. You'll be reunited with the other hostages then, and I expect you're looking forward to seeing your parents.'

'Yes, I am. Do they know I'm here, do you think?'

'Oh, I doubt it, dear. We didn't know that you were really coming out until lunchtime, and you were only allocated to us shortly before you arrived at the InterContinental. They'll know that you're being looked after though, and are coming home first thing tomorrow.'

'Oh, OK.' I must just be patient.

'Hassan,' Mrs Hamilton calls, 'would you show Anna to her room?' Then, to me: 'He'll carry your case for you. I'll see you tomorrow. I'll wake you in good time, at about four a.m.'

I follow Hassan as he pads barefoot down a long corridor in his crisp white uniform. We walk away from the main reception rooms and pass an open door to what looks like a study. Inside, a tall gaunt man with trimmed white hair is writing at an antique desk. Mr Hamilton perhaps.

We arrive at a room at the end of the corridor, still on the ground floor. It's painted white with a wooden bed in the middle covered with an embroidered blue bedcover. There's a shuttered window on one wall, and tall French windows on the other and a door at the end of the bed that leads to a small bathroom.

When Hassan has gone, I stand and look at the deep white bath and its taps with mouths like French horns. The carved basin has soap, talcum powder, toothpaste, shampoo and a pot of cream on the shelf above it. The shiny white toilet flushes. I check.

In the soap dish is a transparent lemon-shaped soap, wrapped in tissue paper. I turn on the tap, fill the basin with hot water and wash my hands, rolling the lemon over and over, making loads of froth. I wipe the suds all over my face and then splash myself, letting the water run down my neck and all over my shirt. I dry myself with the little white hand towel, burying my face in its freshly laundered softness. I hear a faint burst of gunfire far off. It's so frequent that I hardly notice it any more and Mrs Hamilton didn't say anything about it, so I suppose it must be OK. The only thing she did say was that I should keep my windows firmly shut, but maybe that's because of mosquitoes.

I lean over and look in the mirror. My face is clean. Really clean. I lean in closer, look into the eyes. Who are you? Who are you now? I don't recognise the girl staring back. She looks different. Her eyes are wild and a bit frightening. I back away. What have I become?

I feel a great wave of fatigue and go and sit on the end of the bed. And that's when I realise how very alone I am. It's the first time in days. It feels so easy with no one else around to complicate things, but I also feel in turmoil, as though I'm churning around inside an enormous wave of emotion. God knows what will happen when it hits the shore.

I have to try to be calm. I'll have a bath.

But I'm starving again, and I really don't want to have to get dressed again after my bath and eat in the kitchen. I want to stay here. I pluck up the courage to ring the bell by the bedside and wait, sipping water from my bottle.

When Hassan arrives, I ask if I can have my supper on a tray in this room.

'Certainly, miss,' His deep-set eyes rest on my splashed shirt. 'And if you like to put clothes for washing overnight outside your door...'

'Oh yes. Thanks. That would be great. Thank you.'

'Is there anything else I can get you?'

'No, thanks, nothing else.' He closes the door quietly behind him, and I wonder whether he was a Palestinian refugee too when he arrived at Mrs Hamilton's ten years ago; whether he lives here, or in a Jordanian refugee camp. I think of Jamal and the Giant back out there with the planes and wonder what they're doing, how they are, whether they're safe. And I feel so sorry not to have said goodbye, not to have ever said how brave I thought they were.

I put my book and my badge and Marni's letter on the bedside table. Then I undress, wrapping myself in the luxurious white cotton dressing gown I find hanging on the back of the bathroom door. I turn on the bath taps, take my dirty clothes and put them outside the door in a neat pile, then I go outside and sit on one of the wicker chairs on the veranda. The garden feels good, full of life, fertile after the desert. The cool air smells of jasmine and of the wet irrigated earth below the pink-and-white oleander bushes. As I breathe it in, I feel some of the tension disappearing.

I sip the rest of my water, hoping that Hassan will bring me more with my supper, and listen to the minarets around the house take up the call to evening prayer.

Allahu Akbar, Allahu Akbar...

Above the distant noise of running water, I hear cars arriving on the gravel drive. Doors slam, there are murmured greetings. And as the shadows lengthen, piano music drifts from the house.

46

18.00 hrs

I'm lying in the bath with soft water lapping around me. I've longed for this moment, but now it's here, it feels odd. One minute I'm shut up in a plane riddled with explosives, and the next I'm lying luxuriating in a hot bath. No wonder I'm confused. I wonder where David and Tim are, and Rosemary, the captain, Jim ... I'm missing them. What's happening to Jamal – and the plane?

It's not that I *want* company. I definitely don't want to make polite conversation with Mrs Hamilton and her guests, or to spend any more time with strangers, but I feel oddly exposed without the others, without the solid shape of the plane around me, holding me safe. And who would be able to understand that – and what it's been like – but them?

You want to be alone. You want company. You want to be free. You want to be back on the plane. What's wrong with you?

You don't know *what* you want.

Yes, I do. I want Marni and Dad and the boys to be there tomorrow.

Tomorrow! I sigh, and feel my shoulders relax.

I close my eyes and let the peace in the bathroom seep into my bones. Even the sporadic gunfire has stopped.

After a while I add more hot water and decide to read Marni's letter again. It's the perfect moment, so I climb out of the bath, dry my hands and trail watery footsteps across the paved floor.

I shiver and pad back to the bathroom with the letter. When I'm back in the bath, I open the envelope, drop it onto the floor and unfold the page.

My darling Anna,
By now you'll be safely back at school...

My eyes run over her words.

...Until then, my precious girl, missing you and loving
you to distraction,
Marni xxx

Will I really be hugging her tomorrow? Really? *My treasure.* That's what she calls us, her treasures. And the word means so much more, because she's always hidden surprise treasures in our rooms: a heart-shaped stone, a piece of sea-smoothed glass, driftwood shaped like a spoon, a velvety seedpod. They're her sign. They say: be amazed by this. Know that I thought of you.

I'm free, Marni. I try the words out. *I am no longer a hostage.* The words sound truthful, and I feel powerfully relieved, but

I still can't get my head round the idea. I know they say I'm free and going home tomorrow, but I can't trust myself to completely believe it. Just like I wouldn't believe it if someone said, Tomorrow you're going to be hijacked. Somewhere inside my head, the switch that makes sense of everything has been turned to *off*, and it feels awful. It makes me feel sad about everything, and as though I've been permanently cut off from reality.

One evening, to distract me when she was going out, Marni left me her old blue-and-gold copy of *Alice in Wonderland*. It has thick card pages, with tissue paper over the bright illustrations. One of the pictures is of Alice swimming in a pool of her own tears. That's what I'm doing now.

47

19.20 hrs

I eat every bit of the meal Hassan brings on a tray: the slice of melon cut into cubes and sprinkled with ginger and sugar, the roast chicken, mashed potatoes and green beans trickled with gravy, and the apple pie and ice cream melted by the time I get to it. And I feel wonderful. *Replete*. Dad's word. I can see him sitting back in his chair and saying, 'Thank you. Now I am perfectly *replete*.'

Despite the warm bath, Marni's letter and the wonderful food, I'm still edgy and anxious because the gunfire has started up again. And now I can hear the occasional muffled *whumph!* of heavier guns, or are they mortars? Surely someone will come and warn me, if there's something serious going on. Won't they? I wonder if David and Tim are worried too. Where are they now? What are they doing? I bet they haven't been split up. And Jamal and the Giant? Are they out in the middle of it all?

A loud burst of gunfire sets my heart racing. That sounded

close. I sit on the bed, my heart thumping, wishing I could go home *right now*.

I'm desperate to speak to Marni, but there's no point asking if I can phone. I have no idea where they all are.

The clock on the bedside table says eight o'clock. I wander to and fro restlessly past the yellow beam on the wall cast by the bedside light. And that's when I see them. In the white plaster above my bed are two holes, two small excavations. I push my finger into one of the craters. It looks just like a bullet hole.

Has a bullet ricocheted in here? Where from? Through the little window, through the French windows, or has someone been shot in this bed?

Will anywhere ever be safe again?

I sit on the bed, wondering how on earth I'll get through the night now.

48

Sunday 13th September 1970

03.55 hrs

Light sears through the curtains. I turn away, but it's insistent. So I sigh and surface, leaving sleep behind.

The bed feels soft, but strange. Then I remember. I'm going home today! A bird calls urgently from the garden. I struggle upright, reach for my watch and squint into the light. Mrs Hamilton said she'd wake me at four. It's five to. As I yawn and try to shake myself awake, I hear footsteps in the corridor outside.

'Hello. Good morning! Anna?' Mrs Hamilton taps on the door.

'Hello, Mrs Hamilton, I'm awake.'

'Good girl. I'll see you by the car in twenty minutes.'

'OK.' I climb out of bed, find my newly pressed clothes outside the door, wash and get dressed. Then I put the last few things in my suitcase, and my book, badge and letter in my shoulder bag. And I close the door on the little blue room.

Outside the sky is a calm, cool pink, and the garden is full of birdsong. A bee buzzes through the bougainvillea by the front door.

Mrs Hamilton is standing by the car in a floral dress and pale blue cardigan. 'You look like a different girl this morning,' she says, casting an approving eye over me.

'Do I?' I'm still so sleepy.

'Just goes to show what a hot bath, clean clothes and a good sleep can do,' she says, lifting my suitcase into the boot and slamming it shut.

Soon we are humming along through the outskirts of Amman. I wind my window down a little. The air smells of spiced earth.

Mrs Hamilton chats about her dinner party, how well it went. How relieved she was that the guests didn't stay too long, what with the early start.

'Thank you for the lift,' I say, as two women in headscarves cross at the traffic lights.

'Not at all. It's the least I can do, especially when . . .' The car vibrates to a distant *thwump* from behind, sounding like a huge fall of earth.

'Oh dear.' She changes gear to overtake a lorry laden with dates. 'Someone's really caught that one.'

'There seemed to be a lot of gunfire last night,' I say.

'Yes, parts of the city are in absolute chaos. Not near to us yet, but even so . . .'

'Aren't you worried?'

'Oh, we've been in this kind of situation before in various hot spots round the world,' she says matter-of-factly. 'Even if the Syrians on the border don't invade, the whole of Jordan may very well collapse into civil war.' We pass a man sitting side saddle on a donkey, herding sheep in a cloud of dust.

'What if the fighting gets much closer to you?'

'Then I expect the British government will advise us to leave. But I don't believe my time is up yet.' She glances quickly at me before slowing for a roundabout. 'Oh, bother – I keep forgetting to tell Hassan to prepare the Red Room for Mother's visit.'

Suddenly I spot the word *Maani* written above a shop and ask Mrs Hamilton if she knows what it means.

'It's a Jordanian name,' she says. 'From the south, I think.'

A clot of white doves rises suddenly from a rooftop, and my heart soars as I think of seeing Marni and Dad at last.

49

05.30 hrs

Mrs Hamilton strides past a woman sweeping the shiny airport floor with a wide broom. The concourse seems unnaturally quiet. Perhaps everyone else has checked in already? Checked in? I go cold. I can't check in! The hijackers still have my passport.

'Mrs Hamilton! My passport! I haven't—'

'It's all right, my dear,' she says coming to a halt. 'I've got the necessary documentation. They gave it to me yesterday. It'll get you onto this flight to Cyprus, and then the connecting RAF one to London Heathrow.' Relief, then an intense weariness, wash over me. I just want to go back to sleep.

'*Saba cal care.*' Mrs Hamilton greets the man at the check-in desk.

'*Saba cal noor,*' he replies, and the check-in goes smoothly.

As we turn from the desk, I thank Mrs Hamilton for everything.

'It's been a pleasure, my dear,' she says briskly.

At the departure gate, I instinctively put my arms out to hug her goodbye, but she just bends down and proffers me a cool cheek. I kiss it lightly. She smells of rosewater.

'Now off you go.' She smiles at me briefly. I pick up my bag and walk towards the gate, where I turn to wave. She's still there watching, looking, I think, alone and sad. I show the official my documentation, turn and wave once more, but she's gone.

The room beyond is lined with seats and is full of faces that look familiar but seem quite different. Mr Newton is cleanly shaven. Mrs Newton's hair is restored and she's in a mauve dress. Maria, the bald man and the blonde girls stand chatting in a circle, all looking abnormally fresh in clean outfits. Susan and her mother, both wearing blue stripy dresses, have shiny clean hair. They're laughing with Sarah, who is feeding her newly scrubbed baby from a beaker. There's no sign of the crew.

Through the wide glass window, a huge Jordanian Airways plane is being refuelled. It looks wrong too; the wrong shape and colour, the wrong logo, the wrong flag.

I hear footsteps behind me. 'Where did you go?' Tim looks strange as well. He's clean and tidy in a blue T-shirt and brown corduroy trousers. Only his lace-ups are the same. A navy gabardine mac swings half on and half off one shoulder, like a musketeer's cloak.

'Where were you yesterday, Anna?' he repeats. 'I couldn't find you anywhere!'

David arrives. 'Yeah, we thought you'd gone off with the hijackers, didn't we, Tim? Become a fully fledged member of the PFLP.' They're both grinning.

'I was in the last minibus. You'd left before I could catch up with you at the hotel,' I say. 'Where did you stay? Were you together? How's Fred?'

'He's fine,' says Tim. 'We were all together, the twins too. There was a swimming pool. We played water polo till it got dark.' I feel a wave of jealousy.

'And we slept like logs in real feather beds,' David says. 'Well, until this horrendously early start.'

'I had three helpings at supper,' Tim says. 'Did you eat masses?'

'Yes.' I'm smiling. 'I did.'

'Actually, I felt really sick afterwards.' He grimaces.

We fall silent and the pause is full of all that has gone before.

'Were you OK?' David asks me. 'Who did you stay with?'

'I was on my own, with a woman called Mrs Hamilton whose husband is a diplomat.'

'So it was OK?'

I nod; shrug.

Tim looks out at the Jordanian plane. 'Do you think you can be hijacked twice?'

'No,' I say.

'Well...' David ponders the question. 'I suppose—'

'No.' I frown at him.

'Good,' says Tim. 'As we have to swap planes at Cyprus, I'm hoping to count both the flights towards my Junior Jet Club points. The twins think they should give us extra points, because we *should* have been on a BOAC flight. I mean, it's not our fault we were hijacked, is it?'

'No,' I say. 'You should definitely ask both pilots to sign your logbook.'

'Yes, then you've got double mileage,' adds David.

Tim looks pleased. 'OK, I will.'

It feels so good seeing them again.

A Jordanian air hostess offers us a bottled drink from her tray and a slightly greasy doughnut. We take one of each and thank her.

David bites into his. 'Oh, there's no jam. Has yours?'

Tim breaks his open. 'No. Hang on – I'm just going to tell the twins about something.' He gallops off, holding his doughnut in one hand and his bottle in front of him like a sword.

'Funny how the hijackers disappeared.' David takes a swig of his Coke. 'Were the Giant or Jamal with you?'

'No,' I say.

'Sweaty?'

'God, no.'

'Wonder where the crew have got to.' He wipes sugar from his mouth with the back of his hand.

'I saw them going into a different room at the hotel,' I say.

'Being debriefed, I expect.'

I laugh. 'You make it sound like a spy movie!'

'Feels a bit like that. I'm going to really milk it when I get back to school.' I watch him glugging down his Coke. He seems even younger today. 'Damn. Where did that drink go so fast?'

'Here.' I hand him mine. I can't face it.

'Thanks.'

Tim skids to a halt, holding a bag of Liquorice Allsorts. 'You told me you liked the blue ones, Anna, so I saved these.' He holds out a handful.

'Wow! Where did they come from?'

'The man we stayed with last night gave them to me, and some pond water for Fred, and new plants, and a new box. I'll go and get him so you can see.' He runs off again and is back in a flash, carrying a blue plastic box with a lid. He lifts the lid, and there is Fred looking grumpily up from an exotic array of water plants.

'Fred!' I say. 'You're in the Garden of Eden.'

'I know.' Tim strokes his shell. 'He's really happy. You can tell because he's smiling.'

'Is he?'

'You can see he is!'

'Oh, OK. If you say so.'

The twins skid across the polished floor in their socks, shrieking and crashing into empty chairs, bumping into bags and prams. The Jordanian air hostess eventually catches up with them. 'Now,' she says, 'we'll be boarding in a moment, so it's time to put on your shoes and collect your things together.'

The tannoy crackles. '*The Royal Jordanian flight to Nicosia, Cyprus, is now boarding.*' Everyone collects their bits and pieces and we line up by the door.

The thought of being on another plane feels odd – and unsafe. But somehow, despite my heart thumping with anxiety, and by not thinking about it too much, I manage to cross the tarmac towards the solid white steps leading up to the plane's open doorway.

There's no dangling rope here. These steps mean business. They're clamped against the plane. I grip the handrail and smell the paint warmed by the sun, and I'm halfway up when there's a commotion below. The older blonde girl is refusing to board. She's sobbing on her sister's shoulder. Two of the ground crew come over to see what the hold-up is. They beckon to the air hostess up in the doorway. Our embarkation comes to a halt. We all stand frozen, as if in a tableau.

The air hostess pushes down past me with two paper bags in her hand. The older girl is struggling, her breath coming in quick gasps. Now her sister is panicking and crying too. The air hostess sits them both on the bottom step and tells them to breathe slowly into the bags. Gradually their breathing becomes more regular, and the steward at the top of the steps begins quietly to encourage the rest of us up into the plane.

I feel shocked and unsettled, so when I reach the top of the steps, I lean forward to Tim in front of me and whisper, 'Shall we sit together – for old times' sake?' Tim nods and gives me a quick, grateful smile. Then he passes the message on to David.

Once inside the plane, I hesitate. It feels unreal. Otherworldly. But I sit, feeling dazed and distant, between Tim and David, waiting for take-off. The *clunk* of the door shutting makes me feel powerfully claustrophobic. I try to shut it out, to think about open spaces, the sea, wide sandy beaches, anything but being shut in again.

As we taxi away from the clutter of buildings towards the landing strip, I stare out of the window at the wire fencing, the runway lights glowing in the grey light, the line of trees, the drooping windsock, and I think of the other Anna, the one who took off from Bahrain those four long days ago. And I don't know where she is any more. She feels as light and insubstantial as a dust particle caught in the sun, drifting randomly...

I look out at the edge of land and the empty blue sky. Maybe the cold air of England, and normality, whatever that is, will make sense of things. And Marni. Marni will help. In the meantime, I'm between David and Tim once again, their arms touching mine on the armrests. The engines roar before the take-off, the plane shudders, shakes as it speeds up, rises and tilts. The Middle East drops away. We're in the air, climbing once again into the heavens.

Flying to Cyprus - 06.15 hrs (local time)

Breakfast comes: half a grapefruit, bacon and an omelette with grilled tomatoes, a roll, butter and marmalade, orange juice, tea or coffee. I stare at the pale yellow omelette steaming slightly, at the soft, subsiding tomatoes and I break open the bread roll, spread the hard cold butter. But should I save it for later? The three of us approach the meal with reverence, with held-in elbows, so as not to knock each other in the delicate task. The memory of no food still hovers over us. We eat terribly slowly, even David, savouring everything, making it all last as long as possible. I cut the slice of bacon into tiny pieces and chew each one separately. When the air hostesses bring the trolley, Tim asks for tea and adds all our sugars to his cup until the spoon stands upright. Then he spoons the melting sugar into his mouth. At the end, he puts his uneaten marmalade roll into his satchel. 'For later.' Having had so little, everything is important, either eaten or saved. We all keep our plastic cutlery, the salt and pepper. Our trays, when they are collected, hold only empty bowls, wrappings and an empty grapefruit shell.

Just over an hour after take-off, we touch down on the island of Cyprus. And when the plane comes to a halt, we're herded off, and immediately redirected across the tarmac towards a BOAC 707. It looks calm and regal, and has a long thin cloud hanging over it, like stretched pastry.

But at the top of the airline steps I'm alarmed to be greeted not just by air hostesses but also by two nurses and a doctor.

'Do they think we're sick or something?' I say under my breath.

'No, they think we've all gone insane,' David says.

'Well, we probably nearly did.'

As soon as we're airborne and the seatbelt signs have pinged off, we are told we can wander about as we please. There's an air of celebration. Trays of sweets and endless free drinks and crisps are passed round. It all feels a bit forced, as though they need to treat us differently or something awful might happen.

I notice that the doctor and nurses are mingling with the passengers. They spend some time talking quietly to the blonde sisters, who managed to board this time without panicking. When they get to us they ask if we have any aches and pains, or, and they lower their voices, any other worries we'd like to talk about. We all shake our heads solemnly.

When they're gone, David looks pretend-devastated. 'Damn. I forgot to tell them that I've acquired this awful aversion to food.'

'I dreamed I ate Fred last night,' Tim says suddenly. 'Should I have told them that?'

David and I can hardly hold in our laughter.

'No, Tim, that sounds like a perfectly normal anxiety dream. How is he, by the way?'

'He's fine. In fact he's very fine,' he says happily.

Mrs Newton keeps one of the nurses occupied with a blow-by-blow account of what she personally went through during the hijacking, especially having had a headache for days on end. When the nurse is finally released from her clutches, I notice Mrs Newton popping the painkillers she's been given into her handbag and ordering another double gin and tonic.

The captain announces that we can come up to the cockpit in twos and threes if we'd like. Tim and the twins are the first to go, and return crowing with delight. The captain has written copiously in each of their Junior Jet Club notebooks, confirming the exact mileage from Amman to London.

'That's fantastic,' I say.

'We're flying *eight* miles up, you know,' he says.

'No!'

'42,000 feet! Travelling at 600 miles an hour!'

'Amazing! I had no idea!'

The three of them go off to play Scrabble, still talking about Rolls Royce engines and seven tons of thrust.

Throughout the flight, the head steward calls out the names of passengers whose friends and family are already waiting for them at Heathrow. Whenever a new list is announced, a cheer goes up and the cabin goes very quiet. Everyone waits, waits for *their* name.

'Yessss!' a person behind me says delightedly, and another further back, and one in front. Then David, then Tim. When will they call out *my* name? Who's going to be there for me? Where are they?

Where *are* they?

Surely I won't be expected to go straight back to school?

I *can't* go straight back! This is *horrible*, waiting for my name to be called. It's like a raffle, but where I'm the only one holding a dud ticket.

The intercom goes again. I hold my breath. There's no Anna on the list. It's unbearable.

Am I really expected to get on a train at Waterloo and take myself off to school on my own, after all that's happened? I imagine being greeted by my housemistress. She'll try to look sympathetic, make me a cup of hot chocolate – and then tell me to get on with it.

I can't believe that no one is waiting for me! Have they stayed in Bahrain? Or maybe they've gone straight to the new house. God, that means that this time tomorrow I'll be walking through the swing doors into the hall, sitting cross-legged on the floor under the stage, being stared at by staff on the balcony checking my deportment.

I cannot go straight there.

'Come on, Anna,' David says, finishing his second Coke. 'Let's go and visit the cockpit.'

'Really?'

'Yes, come on.'

I sigh. 'OK.' There's nothing much else to do.

The plane is loud with laughter and high spirits. The adults are celebrating their freedom in style. It feels far more like a wedding party than a flight home. I'm amazed at the amount of champagne washing around. A ruddy Mr Newton is standing shouting above the din at Mrs Green, who looks flushed and embarrassed.

Inside the cramped cockpit, the captain and navigator sit among the hundreds of switches lining the space over their heads. I think of *our* captain and navigator. I wish they were in here, flying us home.

The maze of dials flickers and twitches above the two men, and they're friendly enough, but clearly a little bored of explaining how everything works. They ask us our names, show us the ejector-seat button and, on the glowing map of the Mediterranean, where France meets the English Channel. I try to look interested, desperately wanting to feel excited, but until I hear that Marni and Dad are waiting for me, it's difficult.

Why don't they *think* before they read out people's names? Can't they imagine what it might be like for the ones who have no one waiting for them? Don't they check?

'You can see that we're going over France, just east of Paris at the moment,' the navigator is saying.

'It's amazing,' David says. 'Like a giant living map.' But it means nothing to me. These people mean nothing. I'm tired of them. I just want Marni and my dad. I want to get away from everyone else now: the strange captain and navigator, the air hostesses, the doctor and nurses. This plane.

Especially this plane.

After we return to our seats, the steward continues reading out his lists. They are much shorter now, just one or two names each time.

'Are your parents waiting?' David asks.

'Haven't heard yet,' I say, trying, and failing, to sound unconcerned.

Over the next half-hour my name still doesn't come up, and the knot in my stomach grows and tightens, until it feels like a great twisted root.

This is all wrong. I should be celebrating like everyone else.

I'm wrong.

More than anything else in the world, I want them to be there waiting. I get up, go down to the toilet, lock myself in and sob.

51

Approaching London - 10.50 hrs (British Summer Time)

The seatbelt sign in the toilet lights up.

'*Ladies and gentlemen, boys and girls, please fasten your seatbelts. We will shortly be beginning our final descent into London,*' booms the intercom.

I turn the PFLP badge over and over in my pocket. *Please,* I say, *make them be there.*

I wash my face, dry it and scrunch up the paper towel and shove it in the bin. I'll see them all greeting each other, being emotional, reunited. Like watching everyone else's parents coming to take them out from school on a Sunday, when your parents aren't.

I take a deep breath and open the door.

The atmosphere in the cabin is electric.

I wander listlessly back to my seat, struggle past David, sit down and fasten my seatbelt one more time.

David hands me a blank piece of paper torn from a notebook. He's asking for my school address. I write it down automatically. I'll be there in a few hours.

'Thanks,' he says, taking it from me. Then he raises his eyebrows. 'Er ... hello?' I look at him blankly. 'Don't you want mine?'

'Oh. Sorry. Yes, of course.' I tear the bottom off the piece of paper. He writes his and hands it to me.

'Where are you going after this?' he says.

'School, I suppose.'

'God, I'm definitely refusing to go straight back. Going to stall for as long as I can.'

'Me too.' Tim has Fred back on his knee. 'Me and the twins are going to say that we need time to recover from our *nightmares*.' Then, seeing my worried expression, his cheeks dimple. 'Ha, just pretending.'

'Last night I dreamed Lady Mac blew herself up with the plane,' David says.

When I don't respond, he stares at me and then it dawns on him. 'Have I missed hearing who's meeting you?'

'No.'

'Oh.' He looks awkward. 'Someone's bound to be there by the time we arrive, Anna.'

'Course they will,' says Tim.

Easy for you both to say, I think. You just feel sorry for me.

I stare at the ice particles forming on the outside of the window. Above tiny clouds soft as junket, another plane draws its thin white line across the sky.

We begin the descent into London, the engine noise changing from a high whine to a gruffer kind of acceptance. The wing dips as we change direction, curving westwards, and I'm blinded for a second by the sun. For a moment I glimpse the edge of the world, where pale sunlight pools like moonlight on water.

'There's just one more message,' the steward's voice says. 'Anna Milton – your parents may be a bit late.'

My parents! My mother and father! Marni and Dad. They *will* be there!

Tim grins. 'See?'

52

London - 11.00 hrs BST

Down, down we go, slicing through a blanket of cloud resembling newly laid concrete, and the tiny ice crystals on the outside of the window melt away.

I put the badge back in my bag with the other souvenirs of my hijack: the turquoise ticket wallet, the BOAC fan, David's school address, *Wuthering Heights* and even the empty Nivea tin. If I show them when I get back, who would understand how much they mean to me, these treasures?

I open the BOAC fan with its bright turquoise paper folded in flutes. On one side, between borders of roses, is a Canadian Mountie in breeches, a Beefeater from the Tower of London, an African man with a giraffe, a Japanese woman by a pagoda, an Australian with a kangaroo. And there, written in small white capitals across the top of the fan, it says:

ALL OVER THE WORLD BOAC TAKES
GOOD CARE OF YOU

I push my feet into my maroon shoes and tie my hair back into a ponytail with my scarf.

I'm going to see my parents.

I follow David and Tim down the plane steps into a quiet English drizzle and then across the tarmac towards the tall grey airport building. A truck reverses on its way to offload the luggage. Another brings the refuelling line.

It's cold. A familiar cold, a sharpness that penetrates the thin cotton of my shirt. Up on the balcony of the building, I can see lots of small figures, too high to make out any faces. I imagine there'll be hundreds of photographers to battle through, and am glad that this bit, this first bit, seems so calm.

We file slowly into the building and up some lino stairs. Our shoes clomp on the steps. No one speaks.

'This way, please.' Pale-faced ground crew in navy uniforms lead us into another room. Someone ticks my name off a list. We wait, in limbo. I still feel as though I've been unhitched from the real world.

A man speaks to us in a singsong Welsh voice. 'Now we have you all here, and before you meet your families and collect your luggage, we'd like to say how very happy we are to have you all back safe in England.' There's a smattering of applause. 'You are all invited to stay here in the hotel tonight, to relax and recover. There will be supper and free accommodation for everyone. Later a few members of the press will be allowed in. This will be carefully monitored. We hope some of you will agree to a short interview and a photo for both the national press and your local papers.'

We're called up individually. David is the first in our group.

'Here goes,' he says, grinning. 'Bye, you guys.' He kisses me on the cheek and gives me a big hug and then he hugs Tim. I watch him disappear through the door with a spring in his step.

I wait with Tim. When I hear my name next I'm surprised that my parents aren't late. I bend down to kiss him quickly on the cheek. He hugs me tightly and then looks up at me. 'Anna –' he's scrabbling in his pocket – 'I saved this for you.' He hands me his last Polo mint. 'To eat when you get to school.'

'Oh, Tim.' I well up. 'That is *so* kind. You are the loveliest boy – remember that.' I turn away tearfully and walk in a daze towards the door.

The room beyond is ugly, fluorescent strip lighting glares overhead. In front of me shapes fall away, shadows lift, shift, and in the crowd I see her hair, her eyes. I see Marni! And then Dad too! I run towards them.

She folds me in her arms and the weight of the last few days falls away. Marni's soft hands, Marni smelling of Je Reviens. Marni.

She strokes my hair, my forehead, my face. 'My precious girl, my treasure,' she says. 'You're safe. You're safe now.'

I'm finally released to my father, who gives a wry smile before I'm crushed against his newly laundered shirt, just where I want to be.

'That was a close one, Annie,' he says into my hair. I try to answer, but can't.

As we walk out of the terminal building, neither lets go of me. I feel the soft warmth of Marni's hand and my father's strong arm round my shoulders, and I can't stop smiling, and crying.

Marni keeps stopping to gaze at me, to hug me again and again. 'I can't take my eyes off you,' she whispers. 'Can't believe you're really here.'

'They're putting us up in the airport hotel for the night,' Dad says, as he collects my luggage from the pile that has somehow arrived at the far end of the next room.

'I tried to let you know I was OK,' I say at last.

'You did so well, darling,' Marni says. 'When we got here, we bought all the newspapers we could lay our hands on, and there you were! It was wonderful to see you! What hope it gave us!'

'Where are the boys?'

'They're with Auntie Di. We've been staying with her since we got to London. But we had no idea how long you'd be today. Or what might happen. We thought it better to leave them there with her. We've called to update them.'

'Are they OK?'

'Yes, they know you're safe. We'll call them later. You can speak to both of them yourself.'

We go through to the hotel reception. 'Anything happen?' Dad asks suddenly.

'What do you mean?' I'm confused.

'Anyone hurt you?' he says. 'Touch you?'

And I'm back there. Back where I don't want to be. Horrified at Maria's muffled cries, her frantic footsteps, the sobbing.

What can I say? What does Dad want to know?

'Um . . . No. Most of the hijackers were nice,' I say. 'But one girl got a bit hysterical at the back of the plane one night . . . Someone –' I stop, disorientated. 'Someone . . . one of the hijackers . . . touched her.'

'My God!' It bursts out of him.

Marni lays a hand on his arm, as if to remind him of something. He nods, calms himself. 'Well, you're safe now, Annie,' he says. And he takes my face in his hands and kisses the top of my head.

Yes, I'm safe. I hear the words, but I don't feel safe. Not yet.

It's like I have a lot of *unsafe* to get out of my system first. I am happy though – yes, happy – but my head feels as if it will burst with it all, with everything that's going on inside it. I'm with Marni and Dad. They're talking. I'm answering. But I still feel separate somehow, as if I'm looking out from behind a kind of gauze.

53

12.30 hrs

We check into the hotel and go up in the lift to the modern family room they've given us on the fourth floor. It has a double bed, a single one in an adjoining room and a bathroom. I look at my little bed with my suitcase already on it and listen to my parents' low voices in the next room. Then my father comes in. 'Look what I've just found, pushed under our door,' he says, smiling. 'It's addressed to you.' He hands me a little brown envelope. It has *Post Office telegram: no charge for delivery* written across it. Typed below that, it says: *Anna Milton – Arriving from Amman Hijack plane Passenger Heathrow airport.*

I tear it open. Inside are two strips of paper pasted across the page and a purple ink stamp from earlier that day.

= WELCOME BACK BABY HOPE YOU HAD
FUN WITH THE GORILLAS
LOVE = ALI FI SPUD AND JAFFA +
SENDER REQUESTS GORILLAS SPELT LIKE IT

I smile and pass it to Dad and Marni.

'What friends—' Marni says, but is interrupted by a knock on the door.

Dad opens it to a tall young man in jeans with shaggy hair and a camera round his neck. 'I'm an authorised photographer, sir,' he says, showing a piece of paper. 'Would you consider a picture?'

'Of course, certainly.' Dad stands aside to let the man into the room, and introduces Marni and me.

'Been a tough few days for you all,' the man says, smiling.

'Slight understatement.' Dad laughs. 'It really was touch and go at times, so we're absolutely delighted to have Anna back.'

Touch and go. Is that how it was?

'Are you glad to be home then, Anna?' the man asks.

'Yes,' I say.

'And how would you sum up your experience?'

Sum up? I hesitate. I don't want to sum it up. 'I can't,' I say. 'Not yet.'

A look passes between Marni and Dad.

'I'm sorry,' I say, feeling useless, my hand feeling instinctively for the Polo mint and the badge in my pocket.

Marni stands. 'If you want to take the picture now, then I think after that we'd like to give Anna a little space to recover.'

'Of course.' The man looks disappointed.

It's probably his first assignment, I think vaguely, but I don't want to answer questions. I can't make sense of it myself, so how am I meant to 'sum it up' to a stranger?

The man arranges two chairs with their backs to the TV in the corner. Marni and I sit on them, and Dad stands behind. Marni holds my hand. Dad has a hand on each of our shoulders.

The flash explodes. Wherever I look, I see blinding bars of white light. They lock in the man's face, his camera, his body, the patterned carpet, the window. And I'm back there – in the desert with the guerrillas, hemmed in, lying under the seats.

I blink. I am not in the desert.

'Just one more,' says the man. 'Smile, please, everyone. Say *cheese*.' Oh my God, *cheese*, I think, as the bars explode again.

Dad ushers the photographer to the door and stands chatting to him. Marni and I wander away to sit on the sofa. *She's right here beside me.*

'I've rung school, by the way,' she says, 'to say you'll be back in a few days. Think you probably need what the army would call a bit of R&R – rest and recuperation. That's exactly what the school secretary thought too.' Suddenly Marni seems distracted, as if she's forgotten something, and I see how tired she is too.

'And . . . ?' I say, smiling.

'Yes, sorry.' Marni comes to. 'And so I thought the best place to do that might be down with Birdie on the farm in Cornwall. What do you think?'

'I think it's a great idea. How many days?'

'Shall we say three or four?'

'Four,' I say.

'OK, five then.'

I laugh. 'I love you, Marni.'

'And I do you,' she says. 'So much. We just need to get down there, don't we? Then we can really relax. It'll be good for all of us. Just think, a lie-in, the farm, Cornish food and air.'

'And peace,' I say.

'And peace.'

Dad closes the door on the photographer. 'Thought I'd check the news,' he says. 'OK?' He pulls the chairs away from the TV and turns it on. The screen flickers. The sound is turned right down.

'Oh God,' I say. My plane is there on the screen with the two others in the desert.

My plane. In the heat, the dust, the wind. The silence.

Suddenly a black puff of smoke erupts from the plane's nose, followed by a huge explosion, blossoming black, bright orange, red. Debris spirals high in the air. A second explosion tears into the main body, ripping it open. The broken tail bursts outwards. Thick black smoke rolls along the ground and into the sky.

'No!' I cry. 'No!'

Tyres explode, plastic blisters and melts. The frame, the doors, the fuselage writhe and twist in white heat.

My plane...

'Good lord,' my father says, stunned. 'The hijackers have blown it to smithereens. Why?'

We stand watching as the flames lose energy. The smoke rolls off. The air clears. The camera zooms in. And all that's left is a black, twisted wreck.

I feel the earth shift.

My mind translates the images, but I feel that it's me that's disintegrated.

That Anna, the one in the desert, has been destroyed, annihilated. Like the plane, she no longer exists.

Dad snaps off the TV, but the image of the plane is still there, exploding, blistering, writhing...

'Marni,' I whisper. 'Help.'

She puts her arms around me, holds me. 'What?' she says.

'What is it?'

'I don't know...who I am.'

'You will,' she whispers into my hair. 'You will find yourself again.' We are both crying softly. 'You will be safe Anna, and calm Anna again. I promise...'

And I look up into her dark eyes, and I believe her.

Epilogue

I went back.

I went looking for the Revolutionary Airstrip in the desert outside Amman, where I'd been held hostage on board a plane for four days.

At first I just Google Earthed it, typing in *Dawson's Field hijackings*, and found it just outside the town of Zarqa, north of Amman on the way to the border with Syria. Dawson's Field is the name of the disused airstrip once owned by the British, a wide flattened strip of desert between a small escarpment and a line of hills. The hills I'd sat looking at while the deadline ticked closer.

I printed more maps, zooming in and out, and, as I studied them, became haunted by the ghost of the old airstrip lying quite clearly there, running east to west, its track marked out in the sand, unerasable, like an archaeological site or a burial mound. To the immediate left of it were two white-roofed buildings and a perimeter fence of some sort around a small network of roads, and an entry gate at the southern end.

I emailed the British Embassy in Amman and asked the concierge at the InterContinental Hotel about the possibility of gaining access to the airstrip, and was told that Dawson's Field was right in the middle of a military zone and that I wouldn't get permission to go in. Perhaps they were jittery about the proximity to the border, where hundreds of thousand of Syrians were gathering, fleeing the civil war that was raging there.

I *will* go back, I thought. I *will* find it. I will stand there on the sand and look out on those hills again.

But I didn't book the air ticket. I made excuses. I didn't have time. It was the wrong season. And still the landing strip haunted me.

One day I wrote down a list of all the feelings I had about returning to Jordan. I wrote quickly and honestly, and found they were entirely contradictory: half positive, half negative. One half were those of a curious woman who was delighted at the thought of an adventure, looking forward to the challenge, to experiencing new sights and discoveries. But the other half belonged to a frightened child. She was hiding inside, looking out through a window, terrified. So I imagined the woman standing alongside the small child. And in my mind's eye I saw her gently put out her hand and say, *Come on, let's do it together*.

'*Please return to your seats and fasten your seatbelts while we travel through Israeli airspace,*' says the voice over the intercom. Why? To stop demonstrations of anguish by Palestinians travelling over the homeland they are forbidden to visit, or because there's a danger of stray missiles? Three-quarters of those now living in

Jordan were originally Palestinians, from several influxes: the first in 1948 when Churchill and the French carved up the area, then after the Six Day War. And more recently there have been more refugees, from Iraq and Syria.

We are flying into Queen Alia airport, named after the late king's wife, killed in an air accident. It's newly built, designed by Norman Foster. It was not there in 1970, when Amman, built on seven hills, was much smaller. The InterContinental Hotel, where we were taken after our release and where I have now booked to stay the night, has expanded and been refurbished several times since my hijacking. Nothing will look as it did, but perhaps I will be able to experience some of the feelings I felt then, some of the constants in Amman life and the locality that I must have seen all those years ago. The overarching feeling I remember of my ordeal is of being alone. But look, I'm not alone now. I'm with my husband of thirty years. He's here beside me, holding my hand.

I look out on blue sky and broken cloud and a great expanse of sea below. Ice particles cluster round the edges of my window. As we drop down, I see a haze of red dust and brown sand with crooked paths and cracked ravines, rising mounds, soft folds, a meandering dry river bed, the shadow of clouds on land. The reddish brown sand stretches all the way to the horizon. As we descend closer to earth, ripples appear, strange scratch marks, a beaten track, hard and clay-covered.

We hit the tarmac and I feel a great surge of emotion. Tears fall.

We climb down the steps and walk towards the new airport, all glass and concrete. Like a collision of sea and sky, its scalloped roofs, shaped like camels' lips, rise and fall.

In no time we're in a taxi flying past olive groves, fruit and vegetables grown in polytunnels, wide expanses of scrub, new highways, tent encampments, men picnicking on the central reservation. There's Louis Vuitton, Starbucks, Ikea and everywhere building works, more building works, more hollow-eyed, unfinished houses. The seven hills of Amman are densely covered with square flat-roofed buildings, fawn and white and all the tones in between. And, as the sun sets below the horizon, the peach sky leaves us for greying clouds and night.

I'm in the foyer of the InterContinental again all these years later, no longer one of a frantic crowd of released hostages being stormed by the media. People sit about unconcerned, lifts ping open, there's background music and bellboys in uniform, an Arab with a bird of prey on his arm, glass cases displaying jewellery, grey-suited security men. The polished floors reflect and shine. I sit in a carved lacquered chair and watch the revolving door turn its circle. I look at the reception desk, at the public phones, at a sofa covered in a rattan rug, like the ones we had at home, and I feel numb.

As we settle into our room, I'm aware of the arrival of difficult feelings. I can't stop thinking about my parents. Both of them dead now, but back then, when I was released and came here, they were all I could think about. How could I let them know I was OK when I didn't know where they were, whether they were going to meet me in London? Whether anyone was. I couldn't even find out if they knew I was alive. There were no mobile phones, and I couldn't call them on a landline as I didn't know where they were. My overriding feeling then was of being alone, and now I seem to be reliving it, as well as feeling an unbearable sense of loss.

The next morning, I stand looking down from the hotel room, seven floors up. I can see twin minarets and a mosque with a pale blue dome decorated in beautiful patterns. And right below me, on a rooftop by a satellite dish, a Siamese cat rolls in the sun from one side to the other, and back again. And there, below it, leaning against a palm tree, a man in a suit is smoking – in the exact way my father did, the same stance, the same way he held his cigarette a little way from him, the same turn of his head to release the smoke. I see them everywhere, the ghosts of my parents: the edge of my mother's chin in the lift, the back of her head in the bar, her turquoise dress. It's taken me by surprise how much they're here – when they weren't before.

We breakfast on fresh fruit and slabs of Jordanian yoghurt. There are bowls of oranges, lemons, overflowing mint, tomatoes and great chunks of halva looking like layered cliffs.

It's time to go and talk to the driver we've hired for three hours to take us, we hope, to Dawson's Field. I don't know what to say, so I ask to go in the direction of the new Hashemite University, and, as we get talking, I gradually mention the reason for our trip. He seems unfazed. His name is Salah, a smart-suited, middle-aged man with an open, friendly face and laughing eyes. He says we can stop and look at my maps when we're outside the town of Zarqa.

He stops under a road sign. It says Syria straight on, right for Saudi Arabia and Iraq. We study the maps. It *is* a military zone, he says, and my heart plummets. I steel myself for disappointment. 'But I think this –' he points – 'is a sort of military club.'

'Really?' I feel a glimmer of hope.

'We shall see,' he says. 'Maybe we can get in there.'

'How?'

'Come,' he says, getting back into the car, 'we shall try. I think I know someone who works there.'

He drives on and then turns off the motorway onto a smaller road leading into the military zone. Army equipment lines the road, there are lookout towers, flattened areas of sand and heaped car tyres that look like makeshift rifle ranges. There's lots of barbed wire. We see a military checkpoint at the far end of the road and Salah turns round quickly. Suddenly he swings right and stops outside a pair of black gates that have armed security personnel standing both outside and inside. 'The Polo Club,' he says, winding down his window. He shakes the guard by the hand. There's an amicable exchange in Arabic. He takes out his phone as if to call his friend. The guard stops him and waves us through.

We're in.

'What did you say to him?' I ask.

'I said that you had heard of the Polo Club and had come all the way from England to see it.'

I'm smiling. 'You're a genius,' I say.

He shrugs matter-of-factly. 'Well, you have to lie sometimes.'

We drive along a narrow road bordered by newly planted trees and park next to a long low white building with high windows. A solemn young man in fatigues emerges from the building and greets us.

We are shown around, first through the long white stable block, empty but for a couple of polo ponies. It's cool inside, almost gloomy, with just a brilliant patch of sun at the far end where the other open door is. It smells wonderfully of horses, and sawdust and hay. We walk slowly down the length of the building, asking questions about the horses. Salah acts as our interpreter. I go over to talk to a beautiful chestnut that hangs its head outside the stable door and whinnies. I ask if it has a name, and I am told it is called *Gazelle*. Tears well up behind my sunglasses. It is what, in the quiet of my mind, I call my eldest daughter.

My husband asks questions while I compose myself. Then I ask if I can take photos on my phone. I can. We are joined by another stable hand – a Pakistani with intense eyes and thick black hair. He's open and patient, answering our questions about the polo ponies with pride. There are ninety thoroughbred Arab polo ponies, he says, for use by the military and the police, and several others stabled privately, some for the King of Jordan.

We pass outside into the light. I can see the low white buildings in the military zone next door that looked like silos on Google Earth. To our right are a number of pens and paddocks, one the whole length of the stable block, full of mares and young foals. The mothers crop the green hay off the beaten earth floor. The little ones suckle. Occasionally one of them is spooked, bucking and cantering to another part of the paddock. They are beautiful. Their flanks shine, their bodies are lean and well muscled, their manes cropped short. Tails swish. The continuous sound of cropping ponies fills the air.

I take pictures, but I feel disorientated, worried that the polo ponies will distract me, that I won't be able to hold on to why I'm here. We come to a white wall at the end of the track with a solid gate we cannot see through. The gate is pulled back and we pass inside. This paddock, we are told, holds the ones bred from English polo ponies. They have to be kept separate from the Arabs. They don't get along well together. They probably don't speak the same language, I say, unthinking. Salah interprets and the men laugh. The ponies, the man in fatigues says, are left out in the paddocks through the winter to make them strong for the game. He puts his hand to his heart when he says strong. They play four to a team in the beating sun.

I walk in among the polo ponies, right into the middle – and suddenly I see my hills. I know them. I cannot believe I am here. These are my hills, this is my place. I feel amazement and disbelief. I feel exhilarated and disembodied. This is the place where I sat in the plane for four days while the deadline ticked away. This is where I walked in front of hundreds of reporters to have my picture taken, here, under the nose cone of the VC10. In this valley, between the running hills to the south and the sharper incline to the north, three huge passenger airlines sat in the heat of the desert trussed with explosives. For four days, this was the epicentre of the world's tension.

And there is no trace. No twisted debris, just the quiet ponies and the low talk of the men behind me. And as I stand there under the huge blue dome of the sky, a small whirlwind starts up. Approaching from the east, it grows, twisting into a funnel, gathering momentum and swirling in through the open paddocks towards us. The ponies seem unconcerned, as the whirlwind stirs up the sand about them, blowing itself out before it reaches us.

I study the landscape. The ground is hard, impacted sand with scrub and scattered rocks. A good place to land a plane. I remember the faint ghost of the airstrip running across the Google Earth map, and I know it really was here that I came in that VC10 out of the sky to the east, to land amid the rising red dust and to taxi into the plane's last position.

They ask if we would like to see the polo pitch, and we walk in hot sunshine along the avenue of paddocks parallel to the airstrip, stopping occasionally to stroke a stud horse, to take its picture. I lag behind, taking film of the hills, panoramas of the place that had enclosed me, that I had looked out on from within.

The polo pitch, the new grass one, is irrigated with water every night, they say. And the grass is luscious: a huge wide flat expanse of it, a lawn on my airstrip. There are hedges, a pavilion with bougainvillea climbing up it; birds chirrup in the lines of newly planted olive and palm trees and in among the shrubs. It is fecund. There's an enclosure to tether polo ponies, a shady pergola for the riders to wait in, and grass . . . so much grass. Did you have to bring new earth in order to plant this grass? I ask, needing to know if my footprints are still under there. Yes, they say, we did.

I leave the men talking and walk out into the middle of the polo pitch. Did I walk here then, across this space? Perhaps to get to the line of minibuses that finally took us away into Amman to be released to the InterContinental Hotel? Were they parked here, on this spot? Or is this where we had our photo taken with the guerrillas?

Suddenly, as I stand in that flat space, two minarets on the far hillside begin their call to prayer. The song of it washes across the land, the two voices pausing in turn, as if waiting for the other to sing the next phrase. They were not here all those years ago, but have come to claim the land as theirs. The sound of the eternal Arabic words is perfect. The final touch.

Slowly we retrace our steps back to the stable block, where white plastic chairs have been put out, and tea poured into glasses. Three more stable hands join us. It's the famous

Jordanian hospitality, solemn, respectful, polite and full of humour. We drink our tea and are asked to stay for lunch, but sadly we have to move on.

Before I go, I stand watching a beautiful white stallion drink delicately from a trough. He lifts his head and water droplets fall from his soft muzzle. The heat haze shimmers under the midday sun, and little black beetles climb in and out of pockets of sand at my feet. I had no idea that all these years later I would stand here and feel so held by these hills. The benevolent landscape seems to accept me, in peace this time. And the fear that I felt, called to the surface and out into the open air, seems to have lost its power.

I could be wrong, but I think I left it behind on that Revolutionary Airstrip, the one that lies just below the surface of the Jordanian Polo Club.

Postscript

While this story is a work of fiction, it is grounded in a real, life-defining hijack that I experienced when I was fifteen. I was there in the Jordanian desert, sitting in a hijacked plane trussed with explosives for four days, while the deadline approached. I really did travel alone back to boarding school, get my belt caught on a grenade, search through trays looking for food and have my picture taken by the press in the desert.

But for years I never wrote about it. It was only when my publisher encouraged me to try that I started to believe that perhaps it was the right time. I began by researching, realising that I needed to place my story in the historical framework of the real event. So I read about the hijackings, looked online, visited the VC10 plane at the Imperial War Museum, Duxford, and eventually returned to Jordan.

When I began to write, I remembered a great deal, and was overtaken by powerful feelings and strong images, but there were still gaps. Try writing in detail about four days that happened a very long time ago: where and who everyone was, what they were wearing, how they moved and behaved. It's hard recalling conversations that took place last month, never mind over forty years ago, so the conversations and characters in my story are imagined. For example, there was no Maria who might have been assaulted, although there were rumblings, that we 'children' were not allowed to know about, that something untoward might have happened with one of the hijackers. Nor was there a drunken Mr and Mrs Newton, though some of the passengers did have too much to drink when the duty-free was being given out to anyone who wanted it. There was a boy with a terrapin, but I never spoke to him. I did sit next to an older boy at the beginning of the hijack, but he is not the fictional David. And so if anyone on the plane thinks they are being described in these pages, that really is not the case. Any inadvertent similarities are entirely coincidental. I also altered other details for dramatic purposes to enhance the story. This *is* a work of fiction.

There were many other people on that plane in 1970. They will have their own stories to tell. This one is mine.

Acknowledgements

With thanks to Charlie Sheppard, Chloe Sackur, Alison MacLeod and Robert Hull, also to Honoria, Marian, Caroline and Deborah, and to the wonderful friends and family who offered invaluable advice and insight. My special thanks, though, go to Stephen, for his unwavering love and support.